D1095016

Better than Laughter

Chester Aaron

Better than Laughter

Harcourt Brace Jovanovich, Inc., New York

Copyright © 1972 by Chester Aaron

All rights reserved. No part of this publication may
be reproduced or transmitted in any form or by any means,
electronic or mechanical, including photocopy, recording,
or any information storage and retrieval system,
without permission in writing from the publisher.

ISBN 0-15-206950-X
Library of Congress Catalog Card Number: 73-181536

Printed in the United States of America
First edition
B C D E F G H I J

For Margaurite Kelly and Louis Segal

Financial and moral support from the Chapel-
brook Foundation helped me complete this
novel and start another. I will be one of the
last writers to thank the Foundation because it
no longer exists. It was one of the less spectac-
ular fatalities of our times.

Better than Laughter

*"Anger is better than laughter:
because in the sadness of the
countenance the mind of the
offender is corrected."*
—Ecclesiastes 7:3

An Introduction

The redwood trees were there, along the northern coast of what is now called California, the day Christ died. They were un-named then and, except for a few Indian tribes such as the Pomos and the Karoks, unknown. They were not to be seen by the eyes of a white man for another eighteen centuries.

Fifteen hundred years after the death of Christ, when Columbus sailed west from Spain, thousands of those same trees that had shared the earth with Jesus were still standing. A million more had joined them. The lumber obtained from a single one of those ancient giants . . . had redwood been suitable for the building of ships, which it wasn't . . . would have made twenty or thirty *Santa Marias.*

Approximately two and one-half centuries after the death of Columbus the band of Boston Militia that twice sent the British troops in retreat down the slopes of Bunker Hill was not aware that three thousand miles to the west vast forests of trees rose into the clouds,

3

weaving a roof so dense that it could not be penetrated by the sun.

In an area now known as Redwood County (an area of nine hundred square miles in northern California) these forests resisted the encroachment of man until the early years of the nineteenth century. Then, unable to resist the gears and blades and motors spawned by the Industrial Revolution, the trees fell, exposing the rich dark soil to the sun for the first time in twenty centuries.

And so began the destruction of the largest living organisms to inhabit our continent in the last fifty thousand years. A fate shared by other trees, by plants and birds and beasts and by men: to be destroyed by man with little purpose and no regret.

Of the millions of acres of fertile soil exposed by the destruction of the forests, a portion, for a time, served as farm or grazing land. For a time. Now, in the last half of the twentieth century, much of it lies smothered beneath a blanket of steel and concrete and plastic.

Today, two hundred years after the first white man entered the redwood forests, there are fewer than a hundred redwood trees in all of Redwood County. One of those trees rises over a corner of the Redwood County Dump, shading two barely upright buildings in which the Dump Attendant, Horace Butright, lives and works.

Chapter 1

"Civilization! I hate it!"

With that protest Allan sailed his paperback novel across the room. Three pages fluttered to the floor before the book struck the wall and lost another two pages.

Sam, brooding over his balsawood model of the *U.S.S. Kennedy,* did not respond. He did not even look up.

"Nothing around anymore," Allan said. "Cowboys . . . Indians . . . mountain lions . . . nothing. Just crummy old civilization."

Flopped onto his stomach, with his hands folded under his chin, Allan stared out the window and across the flagstone patio and the sculptured bushes and the clipped green lawn (being clipped even closer this very minute by Mr. Okano) to the blue water in the swimming pool. Allan had cleaned the pool that morning, but since then the California live oak had dropped more leaves. He'd better remember to clean the pool again this evening, before his father came home.

Remember, Allan thought, *remember. Clean the pool before he comes home, clean the pool before he comes home.* The freight-car words, hooked to each other, traveled round and round the circle of track in his mind reserved for such messages. *Clean . . . the . . . pool . . . before . . . he . . . comes . . . home . . . clean . . . the . . . pool . . . before . . . he . . . comes . . .*

After the words piled up on each other and collapsed, Allan wiped the track clean.

Mr. Okano, scurrying among the azaleas and the rhododendrons, was clipping and tossing bits of branches over his shoulder onto a canvas cloth stretched flat near the pool. What had Mr. Okano's father been like? Had Mr. Okano been afraid of him?

Why, Allan wondered, should *he* be afraid? And no use pretending anymore that he wasn't.

Lying here on a Saturday afternoon, reading, half asleep, he ought to feel relaxed, he ought to feel at peace, he ought to feel pleasantly exhausted after this morning's ball game and this afternoon's long bike ride. Instead, he lay here reading the same sentence over and over again, urging Mr. Okano to hurry, watching the clock on the wall above his desk where Sam was working. His anxiety about his father's reaction when he would get out of his car and walk past the pool was so intense that it could only be called fear. For a half hour now, while he'd been fighting his way through Chapter 5 of *The Mushroom Men from Mars,* Allan had been listening for the departure of Mr. Okano's truck so he could rush outside and clean the pool once more.

If he weren't afraid of his father's anger, he could stroll outside after dinner and clean the pool. Or he could leave it until tomorrow. But that was it, that was exactly it. His father would be angry. He'd walk past the pool and he'd shake his head in silent reproof of Allan's laziness. Well, Mr. Okano would be collecting his cuttings and tools any minute now and going home. His father had never sensed Mr. Okano's possessive pride in the garden. Allan had. He knew too well that Mr. Okano resented anyone else so much as touching a blade of grass in the yard. Why shouldn't he? It was more his yard than it was Allan's or Sam's or their father's.

Just three nights ago, after Harry Collins had served Allan a thick slice of beef, he'd offered, along with the plate, a generous serving of sarcasm. "That's a strange swimming pool we got out there. First one I ever saw that grows leaves."

Allan, knowing there was little chance of convincing his father, had said, again, he had cleaned the pool that morning.

"Well," Harry Collins had said, "it's obvious to me it has to be cleaned twice a day. Can't understand why you couldn't see that. If you *did* clean it this morning."

"He did, dear," Mrs. Collins had said, cupping Allan's chin in her hand and tilting it to receive, in return, a smile. But the smile failed to materialize. "I saw him clean it. Right after breakfast."

Allan had suggested then that maybe Mr. Okano might want to clean the pool. After all, Mr. Okano liked the yard, and he'd designed it and he took care of it and . . .

Harry Collins had pointed a long finger across the bowl of mashed potatoes. "Okano could clean the pool in one-tenth the time it takes you. I know that. But I want you to do it. I've made that one of your few responsibilities around here. I want you to clean it. Is that clear?"

Allan had replied that yes, that was clear.

But it was not clear. It had not been clear that evening and it was not clear now. *Responsibility:* that was one of those words his father used when he was convinced he had a duty to educate his sons. "Making a man of you." That was how his father had described it later, when he'd come into Allan's room to say good night. Having had his dinner and a few follow-up drinks, he was feeling mellow. "All I'm interested in," he'd said, "is raising you right. Making a man of you."

Now, after watching Mr. Okano scurry about the yard, snipping, trimming, dragging a hose from grass to tree to bush, Allan sat up. He considered the effort involved in retrieving his book, and with a very dramatic groan that also failed to distract Sam, he fell back on the bed again.

Responsibility. Why should he or Sam be assigned one responsibility? Why not six? Or ten? Or none? Why should the pool be *his* responsibility? Why not the garage? Or the trash? Or the waxing of one of the three cars?

Neither Allan nor Sam ever asked these questions out loud, of course. Asking them would mean at least one lecture about a child's need for responsibility. And the usual advice that a son's to do what he's told to do. Or there would be the other approach. "Why can't you be like Sam? Sam never argues. Sam does what he's told to do. Why don't you learn from Sam? It's a damn shame a twelve-year-old has to learn from a ten-year-old. Isn't it?"

"No, it's not a shame." That was what he wanted to say, but he never did. He'd not be trapped into either defending himself or attacking Sam. And being twelve years old, he had no right to question authority. So he'd been told, over and over.

Allan's hand, touching the floor, found a sock. He tossed it at Sam but missed. "I wish I was grown up already," Allan said. There was not even a suggestion of a response from the desk, where Sam huddled over the balsawood model.

8

Allan closed his eyes, to watch long lines of soldiers march in perfect step across the drill field. Like soldiers, children are meant to obey, without question, every command. He could hear his mother's soft voice repeating her modest variation of his father's words. "My goodness, Allan, what would our world be like if children made the rules? Now don't be a silly little mouse."

What would the world be like? It would be better, that's what it would be like.

No, no. Boys, being boys and not men, must do as they're told. Period. That's the way it is, that's the way it has been, that's the way it will be. Forever. Parents decide what children will do until those children are parents themselves. "Do this! Do it this way because I say this is the way to do it! No questions! Hup . . . two . . . three . . . four . . ."

"Hup, two, three, four," Allan called in his best drill-sergeant, parade-ground voice. But Sam continued squinting at the *U.S.S. Kennedy.*

Allan, lying on his stomach, balanced his chin on his right fist. "I wish something would happen. Something exciting. Like an invasion by the Mushroom Men."

The novel he'd been reading described the invasion of Earth by Mushroom Men from Mars. Their daily diet of grownups offered exactly those proportions of iron and sugar required by Mushroom Men to survive. But, Allan wondered, what would the Mushroom Men eat once they'd consumed all the grownups? Would they start on children? Were two children equal to one grownup? And what about the Mushroom Boys? Mushroom Men at one time had surely been Mushroom Boys. What did Mushroom Boys eat?

To divert himself from the disturbing answers, Allan spoke directly to his brother. "Sam, are you bored?"

Sam, working quietly, gave no indication he'd even

9

heard the question. The tip of his tongue was out, testing the surface of his upper lip. Whenever Sam concentrated, as he was concentrating now on the *U.S.S. Kennedy,* his tongue kept straying out to lick at his upper lip.

Allan sighed. "I wish there were still cowboys around. And Indians. And wild animals. There used to be all kinds of wild animals right here where we're talking."

"*I* ain't talking," Sam said, daubing a balsawood joint with glue.

Allan considered the urge to walk over to the desk and squeeze the contents of the tube of glue on Sam's head. But he decided to remain where he was, so he'd not disturb the pictures of how it used to be in the fields and hills around this house. Before television. Before houses. Before the roads were here. Before there were human beings. Lions, wolves, grizzly bears . . . all kinds of wild animals had moved across the patch of ground on which this house was built.

Now, during the night, a deer occasionally wandered down from the hills to nibble the buds of the curly willows. Raccoons snarled and growled at the back door on those nights when his father, home early for once, sat on the patio and tossed them crusts of bread or dog biscuits. But deer and raccoons were not wild animals. Mountain lions, grizzly bears, wolves . . . they were wild animals. And they were gone forever.

"I hate civilization," Allan said. "You go to school, you come home, you go to school, you come home. For what? Bah!" He threw his pillow across the room. It landed on top of his paperback novel.

"Momma's gonna give it to you," Sam said, without looking up from his work. "She's already fixed your bed twice today. And there's people coming tonight for dinner."

"*She's already fixed your bed twice today.*" It was a

perfect parody of Sam's voice. "Why don't you make your mess in your own room?"

"The light's better in yours. And you said I could work here."

Allan rolled onto his back again and stared up at the ceiling. "Anyway, I can fix my bed so good Mom'll think Thelma fixed it. I had the neatest, tightest bed in camp all summer. Mr. Montgomery could toss a quarter on it and the quarter . . ."

"I know, I know. It would bounce three feet in the air."

Allan had impressed Thelma when he and Sam had returned from camp. For five days. That was as long as he'd made his own bed every morning. On the sixth day Thelma had inherited the job again. "On the sixth day he rested," Thelma had said. "I knew it was too good to be true."

But she'd laughed when she'd said it. She'd thumped him on the top of his head. He'd winced and she'd hugged him to her, rubbing his head and apologizing for having struck him so hard.

Thelma rarely hugged either him or Sam anymore. When they were babies and they had stayed with her and *her* children, in Oakland, she was constantly hugging them, constantly cooing over them. Well, they weren't babies anymore. That was probably the reason she so rarely hugged them now. She probably didn't hug her own children, Ralph and Rebecca, anymore.

"You know," Allan said, "Thelma's the only one doesn't keep reminding us we ought to be thankful."

Sam refused to accept the bait.

Allan had been sure that either a comment about Thelma or a comment about those daily reminders of their good fortune would stir Sam to some sort of comment.

Good fortune . . . their good fortune to be living in

11

Orchid (where there were never any riots) . . . their good fortune to have such a new and fancy home . . . their good fortune to have an Olympic-size swimming pool . . . their good fortune to have enough money to go to movies two or three times a week if they wanted to . . . their good fortune to never be hungry . . . their good fortune to live in Orchid, to live in California, to live in the United States. Well, if they never appreciated their good fortune, it would not be because they'd never been told. They were told these things every day, two or three times every day, by their mother or their father or their teachers or by Reverend Bonney or by the bus driver or by one of a dozen other grownups.

Why didn't Thelma ever refer to their good fortune? She'd talked about everything else. Or at least she'd used to. Why did their parents never ask Thelma to let them stay with her, anymore, in Oakland? Why didn't Thelma invite them? Why did he and Sam shy away from talking about it to Thelma as if they'd all three made some secret agreement?

Why, when they asked about it, did their parents always change the subject?

They'd not stayed with Thelma, in Oakland, since the Watts rebellion. Their mother and father had said "the Watts riots" until they realized that Thelma always said "the Watts rebellion." That was when they'd decided to not just stop using either word but to stop referring to the incident at all.

Long afterwards, when Allan described a magazine article about "the Watts rebellion," he was given to understand, by a severe glance from his father, that, "riot" or "rebellion," it was no longer a suitable topic for discussion. Actually, it was one of several such topics no longer suitable for discussion. Troubles on the University campus at Berkeley, drugs, the Vietnam War . . . these were topics reserved for adults, and reserved for

12

those times, usually dinner parties attended by his father's partners or potential clients, when Sam and Allan were beyond the range of contamination. Nor was there ever discussion, in their presence, about black people, referred to almost always as Negroes, almost never as niggers.

There was no longer any reference (when they were alone, just the four of them) to Thelma. There used to be. "Thelma is so sweet . . . Thelma is the perfect maid . . . Thelma is the gentlest person you could ever meet, a Christian . . . Thelma has an instinct for children . . . Thelma is like a sister . . . Thelma is like a daughter . . . Thelma is like a mother to the boys . . ."

Allan, shocked by a sudden vision of the Mushroom Men advancing on Thelma, swung his fists at the air. He leaped to retrieve the pillow and the book. He fitted the loose pages in place and returned to his bed, where he tried to read. But his concentration could include no more than three or four words before his mind would wander again to Thelma. What would she say if he came right out tomorrow and asked if he could live with her in Oakland? Sam would be willing. Last Saturday night, on their way home from a movie, Sam had asked, "Do you ever wish we could live at Thelma's?" Before Allan could reply, he'd added, "I'd like to. I like Thelma. I want to ask her about Ralph and Becky, but I never do. I can't. I don't know why, but I can't."

Five Saturdays before that night he and Sam had come home from camp to find Thelma, instead of their mother and father, in the house. They, Thelma had said, just the three of them, would be alone for three weeks. Allan had rushed outside and, with all his clothes on, had jumped into the pool, to be followed by a shouting, singing Sam.

"Three weeks," Sam had shrieked, splashing Allan, "three weeks, three weeks."

Allan had laughed at Thelma's threats to throw a box of soap powder and all their dirty clothes in the pool so they could celebrate and wash their clothes at the same time.

What had happened? When did . . . whatever it was that had happened . . . when did it happen? Was it his fault? Why could he feel no affection or even gratitude toward the man and the woman he knew to be his parents? He did not feel related to them. They might just as well be someone else's mother and father stopping over for the day in this house.

"Want to go to a movie tonight?" Sam asked.

"I don't know. I suppose so. What's playing?"

Sam leisurely opened a new tube of glue. "I don't know."

"So we go to a movie. Big deal."

"What else," Sam asked, touching the tip of the tube to a blade of one of the *Kennedy*'s screws, "is there?" He returned the cap to the tube. "It ain't vacation and we ain't in camp . . ."

"I wish we were. I wish summer vacation was just beginning and we were leaving for camp tomorrow instead of driving around another one of Dad's old projects." Allan spat out the word *projects* as if it were a foul-tasting seed.

"Yeah," Sam said. "Me, too." Apparently uncomfortable with his admission, Sam frowned and stared at his fingertips.

Allan decided against reminding Sam how upset he'd been when their mother had told them they were being sent to camp for the summer. Sam usually accepted disappointments with an aplomb that infuriated Allan, but that day he'd stormed around the house with such sullen anger that even Thelma had been impressed.

All year, before the sudden announcement that he and Sam would be going to camp, they'd been talking

14

about a visit to Disneyland in the summer. If not Disneyland, a trip down the Colorado River on a raft. Or a trip across country with stops at the Grand Canyon and the Petrified Forest and Kentucky's Mammoth Caves. The announcement about the camp had come just two days before school ended, before the summer vacation was to begin. "Best of all," their mother had said, as if this would assure acceptance, "there won't be any grownups around."

They'd been eating breakfast. Sam had pushed his cereal away. He'd left the table and stomped down the hall to his room.

Hiking and fishing and living in the woods had never appealed to Sam. The two times he'd been to Yosemite he'd returned home with blister-covered feet, his body one pink lump of mosquito bites. Despite hours of patient instruction from their father, Sam had never caught a fish much larger than the bait he'd used.

Their father had been sitting to the left of Sam the morning they were informed they'd be going to camp. "I sure wish I could go with you," he'd said. "But parents aren't allowed. This is just for kids. How about that? You wish you were going, Gladys?"

Allan had heard his mother's assurance that she sure did wish just that. And then he'd heard her lie. It was as simple as that: she'd lied.

"I sure do wish I was going. The idea of a summer of parties and dinners and that sort of thing doesn't appeal to me one bit."

That was when Sam had left the table.

Allan, remaining at the table, had watched the shock and uncertainty trade reflections on his mother's and father's faces.

A lie. She was lying. So was his father.

For his mother, Allan knew, the expectation of a summer filled with parties and dinners was far more

15

attractive than a trip to Disneyland or a boat ride down a river or a camp in the mountains.

Though it was Sam who'd most loudly resented going to camp, it was he who'd complained the loudest when the time had come to return home. Even the mosquitoes that summer had seemed to recognize the importance of converting his hatred of woods and fields and lakes to love. Without once being reminded, he'd changed socks every day. His blister-score for the entire summer had been three. Though he was always the last to return when they went on weekend hikes, he'd only laughed and waved at the taunting cries of "Here comes Sam Collins, the fastest turtle in California."

When the camp master had deposited them at the curb in front of their home, they'd trudged up the path with the long solemn faces of prisoners approaching the iron gate that would soon clang behind them. Then they were running through the house, cheering and jumping into the pool. Thelma was there.

And it had been the old Thelma . . . the loving Thelma . . . the devoted Thelma.

She hadn't exactly said she was *glad* they'd be together again, alone, without Mr. and Mrs. Collins, but Allan had known she was. He could sense it. *He* was glad and, he knew, so was Sam.

That night, in a rare moment of such confidence, Thelma had admitted that she wouldn't have considered staying if the Collinses hadn't offered her double salary for the three weeks. "Rebecca and Ralph, they're old enough to stay by themselves now. But, like my daddy say, 'Money ain't everythin' unless you ain't got nothin'.'"

Thelma had been as firm and demanding as she'd always been. But Allan, as well as Sam, had responded to her firmness with a spirit and humor that made even Thelma uncomfortable. "Whatta you boys up to? Home

16

on time every night. Goin' to bed when I say it's time. You even keep your rooms neat almost. What you boys got up your sleeves 'sides a couple dirty arms?"

At night (like those nights when they used to stay with her in Oakland and she'd told them and Rebecca and Ralph stories about her childhood in Arkansas) they'd sat together, usually in Sam's bedroom, and she'd told those stories again. On Saturday nights she'd let them stay up past midnight so they could watch the late movie on TV. As thrill surrendered to horror, they'd all huddled together, reassuring each other that there was nothing to worry about. But before going to bed, they'd marched through every room in the house, checking closets and doors and windows.

The Collinses had returned in late August, a week before school started. Allan's father was home for one day. Then he was gone for three, to inspect those projects that had worried him while he'd been lying on the beach at Waikiki.

Allan dropped *The Mushroom Men from Mars* on his bed. Thoughts of tomorrow's picnic had stifled all interest in reading. "Boy," he said, "Saturday's so close to Sunday, it's the second worst day in the week."

A thin film of perspiration covered Sam's nose and forehead. Had he even heard Allan's comment?

"I think we ought to do something exciting," Allan said. He sat up. "Sam, I have a idea."

"Yeah?" And Sam scratched his head, contemplating a bulge that had just emerged on the carrier's flight deck.

"No, you really have to listen."

Sam resisted for a moment and then, sighing, he capped the tube of airplane glue. He swiveled on his . . . or rather on Allan's . . . chair and he faced his tormentor.

"Sam, are you sort of . . . well, just sort of bored all the time?"

17

Sam's eyes threatened to drift back to the carrier, but Allan insisted. "Aren't you? Come on. Tell the truth."

"Bored?" Sam squinted, as if the word were a bright light that hurt his eyes. "Oh, I guess so. Yeah. But, well, not all the time."

"OK, let's do something. I mean really *do* something."

"Like what?"

"Like . . . run away. Let's run away. Let's go to sea. We can be cabin boys like Jim Hawkins. Remember? Or we can join the circus. Be lion-tamers. Or tightrope walkers. Or trapeze artists."

"Me? On a trapeze? Uh-uh, not me."

"Well, let's just run away."

"Why run away? Run away from what?"

"Run away from . . ." and Allan waved his hand in a gesture that included the house, the town of Orchid, the people in the town, the whole world . . . "from everything."

"But Mom would cry and Dad would . . ."

"Dad would what? I bet we could be gone for a week and no one would notice. Thelma would, maybe. She wouldn't have to clean our rooms or make our beds. But no one else . . ."

"Aw, that's not true, Allan. You're exaggerating. You always exaggerate."

"OK, so I'm exaggerating a little. But you know it's almost true. Don't you? Admit it, Sam. What would Dad do if he found out we'd run away?"

"Well . . ."

"Come on. What would he do?"

"He'd feel bad. They both would."

"Big deal. Wow! They'd feel bad." Allan would have been harsher in his criticism, but when he saw

18

Sam's eyes begin to mist, he felt sorry, as always, for his younger brother. He decided to be merciful. Some day soon he might not be so easily stricken by the sight of tears in Sam's eyes, but today wasn't the day. He went to his desk and feigned more interest than he really had in the carrier's plans. "You know what, Sam? If someone tells me . . . just once more . . . just *once* more . . . that I ought to be glad for what I've got and I oughtn't to complain and a million kids are starving in Asia and I should be ashamed of myself . . . you know what I'm going to do?"

"What?" Sam asked, his face lighting up at the prospect of Allan delivering one of his exotic images of destruction.

"I'll . . . I'll . . . I'll spit in his eyes."

Sam burst out laughing, and Allan, realizing how preposterous his image had been, succumbed. He laughed, too.

But even as Allan laughed, he knew that Sam was disturbed. He saw Sam glance down at the *U.S.S. Kennedy*. Was Sam remembering now that for two weeks he had been waiting for their father to fulfill his promise to help build the ship?

Allan had not expected any dramatic response to his suggestion. He certainly had not expected the response that occurred now in himself. He heard his own words as if someone else were speaking to him, as if someone else were urging him: *run away . . . run away . . . run . . . away . . .*

"Yeah," Allan said. "Let's run away." He leaped onto his bed, doubled up his pillow, and punched his fist into it. "Come on, Sam. Let's run away."

Despite the firm shake of his head, Allan could tell that Sam was tempted. Today was Saturday. Tomorrow, Sunday, they would spend the day on another one of

19

those so-called picnics! There was never wrestling on the grass or riding Ferris wheels or playing ball or swimming, but his dad always called it *a picnic*.

Stuffed into two or three cars with the usual friends or the usual partners, they'd spend the day touring the hills and valleys where their father's company, Collins Construction, was erecting apartment-house projects or shopping centers or parking towers.

To Allan, the top of one hill, sliced away and seeded with rows of houses, looked like the sliced and flattened top of every other hill seeded with rows of houses.

His father would lead the parade of admiring partners and friends over redwood patios, past splashing fountains, through flower-bordered shopping malls. Everyone would take turns photographing and being photographed. The meaningless jargon of their father's narration would push Allan and Sam lower and lower in the seat, where they would remain, somber and silent, until their father would ask them if they liked this or liked that. One of them, usually Sam, would respond with a simple "Yeah" or "Uh huh" or "That's cool, Dad."

Interpreting their restraint as awe, Allan's father would pat their shoulders or cuff them playfully on the cheeks. Or he'd wink and say, "Whatta you think of your old man, huh? A truck driver just ten years ago and now look at him. Another five years, fellas, and I'll retire and we'll all travel around the world five, six, seven times a year. How about that?"

Tomorrow, Allan thought, another Sunday meant another such picnic. And Sam *had* to be thinking the same thing. He *had* to be.

"Where would we run to?" Sam asked.

"Just run, that's all," Allan said. "There's all kinds of places."

"Like where?"

20

"Like, well, like Gualala. Hey, yeah, what about Camp Gualala?"

"Way up there?" Sam winced and swallowed hard. "It took three hours to get there by bus. How long would it take by bike? We would take our bikes, wouldn't we?"

"Sure. A day, maybe, maybe two. So what? It doesn't matter. We're running away. We don't have to worry about time. We can sleep in barns or under bridges or places like that where people always sleep when they're on the lam."

"On the what?"

"On the lam. Means when they're on the run."

The idea was obviously more appealing to Sam now. "Hey, there won't be anyone at camp. We'd be all alone."

"That's right. No one will know we're there. The half tents will still be up, though. We can live in one of them. There won't be any cots, but we can take our bedrolls. We know where the apple trees are. And the nuts. And the berries. You can live on apples and berries and nuts. Daniel Boone did. Indians did, too."

"And you can fish," Sam said. "While you fish, I can pick berries."

They continued elaborating on their plans for their existence in the forests until Allan happened to glance at the clock. His father would be home soon. He rushed outside, Sam at his heels. With Sam's help, he had the pool cleaned in ten minutes.

They decided, after much discussion, that they ought to go to the Saturday night movie. If they didn't go, someone might get suspicious. They ate an early and hasty dinner (while their father napped), and then their mother drove them to Main Street, to the Orchid Theater. When she left them off at the curb, she reminded them that they either had to walk home or take a bus because there would be guests for dinner and she'd not be able to leave the house. Now that Thelma no longer worked on Saturday nights and Mrs. Collins had to take whatever domestic help the agencies sent her, she was spending more of her own time shopping and preparing dinners. "I'll be running all evening, and this is an important dinner party."

Allan was not impressed. To his mother every party was an important party. Dinner parties and guest lists occupied as much of her time as Collins Construction Company, Incorporated occupied his father's. "You're my public relations firm," his father had said once, hugging her. She'd rested her cheek on his shoulder and beamed. "It's the least I can do," she'd said. "You work so hard. I wish I could help more than I do."

Midway through the second movie, Sam could endure it no longer. He had to leave. "Tomorrow," he said. "All I can think about is tomorrow."

"You want to hitchhike home?" Allan said when they left the theater.

"Mom said we couldn't ever hitch," Sam said. He caught the grin on Allan's face, and he stepped out into the street. "OK."

When the boys went to bed, their father left the guests to come into their rooms to say good night. After spending about ten minutes with Sam, he sat on the edge of Allan's bed. "I bet you'll have fun tomorrow," he said. "After church we're all driving to Bolinas, to a ranch I'm thinking of buying. After the trees are cut down, there's going to be fifty houses built. Wait and see. You'll love it. Hundreds of fir and redwood trees eighty, ninety years old. Some of them maybe a hundred. We'll leave lots of them, too. You can't just cut down all the trees. Not anymore. Ecology. Then, on the way home from Bolinas we're gonna stop someplace else. I won't tell you where or what it is. But I bet you'll be surprised. The county

22

supervisors signed the contract three days ago. Everything's ready to go. It'll be the biggest, most important job we've ever had. This will put Collins Construction Company on the map." Harry Collins rumpled Allan's hair and hugged him. "The pool's in perfect shape," he said. "Clean as a hound's tooth." He gave Allan an extra squeeze and, for the first time in months, pressed his lips to Allan's cheek.

Allan resisted the urge to throw his arms around his father. After frequent and prolonged experience with anger and suspicion and resentment, the temptation borne of a brief moment of love could not be trusted.

No sooner had his father gone from the room than Sam, in his pajamas, came racing down the hall and onto Allan's bed.

What would happen tomorrow, Sam wondered, when their parents discovered them missing.

"They'll call the police."

"And then what? What will the police do, Al?"

"Oh, there'll probably be search parties. Maybe radio announcements. Things like that."

Completely caught up now in the promise of adventure, Sam was more excited than Allan. "Wow! Just like in the movies." How long did Allan think they could go without being caught?

"Weeks. Months, maybe. Maybe we'll never get caught."

Never? Sam grew suddenly sober. Never? They'd come home sometimes, wouldn't they? They wouldn't stay away forever, would they?

"Oh, when we're grown up, yeah. We'll come home when we're grown up."

What if they were caught? What would happen? What did Allan think their father would do?

"What'll he do? He'll yell at us, he'll tell us we don't appreciate anything. He might even spank us. Or maybe he won't let us go out for a month. Well, if we do get caught, whatever he does it'll be worth it just to get away."

How far did Allan think they could go on their bikes in one day?

Allan was two grades ahead of Sam and had never had less than an A in math. He calculated now that in twelve hours . . . using the back roads . . . staying off the main highways and the freeways . . . with their ten-speed Schwinns . . . in twelve hours they ought to be able to make sixty or seventy miles at least. And seventy miles was halfway to Camp Gualala.

"Allan."

"Yeah?"

"You won't do like you do sometimes, will you?"

"What do you mean?"

"I mean, you know, get so far ahead of me."

"I promise, Sam."

That did it. Sam bounced on the bed until Allan reminded him that they had to be careful and not let their mother or father suspect anything. They also had to get plenty of sleep because tomorrow would be a hard day. Sam stopped bouncing, but he did not leave the bed.

"How much money have you saved?" Allan asked.

"Three dollars and forty cents. You?"

"Six dollars and twelve cents. We could go a long way on that. Probably clear to . . . to Chicago if we wanted." They shared the dark silence, and then Allan said, "You better move fast when I wake you. We'll have to get away before Dad gets up."

"I'll get up right away. I promise."

"You always go back to sleep."

"I won't this time. You watch."

Sam slipped off the edge of the bed and went to the wall, fitting himself into the shadows of the oak tree thrown on the wall by the moonlight.

24

In the morning the birds would be singing in the branches of the tree. In another few weeks the leaves would all be gone. The shadows of the branches would dance on the wall, like those cardboard skeletons sold on Halloween, but he wouldn't be here to see them.

Sam moved past the wall, stopped to trace the shape of a branch with his finger, and then left the room.

When the alarm rang, Allan grabbed the clock and stuffed it under his pillow until he could find the button that turned off the alarm. He waited. The sun had not come up yet, but the dark sky in the east was flaked with gold.

Allan rubbed his eyes. It's Sunday. No school. *School!* He threw off the blanket and rushed, on tiptoes, into Sam's room. "Sam," he whispered. "Sam. Get up. Remember?"

Sam mumbled, dug his face deeper into the pillow, pulled his blanket over his head, and then sat up. He would have shouted had Allan's warning . . . a hand pressed against his lips . . . not come just in time. "We're running away," Sam whispered from behind Allan's hand. Allan nodded and said that Sam had better hurry. Sam sat there, blinking and scratching his belly. "We better take sweaters, Al."

"OK, but hurry."

Sam promised he'd hurry, but he remained there, blinking and scratching. Allan said he'd be in the kitchen, waiting, and Sam had better hurry or he'd leave without him. Sam leaped out of bed.

Allan carried his bedroll and his fishing pole (in its canvas jacket) and his blue sweat shirt (*U.C.—Berkeley* stenciled across the front) to the kitchen, where he slapped several cheese sandwiches together. Once, forgetting his advice to Sam, he slammed the refrigerator door. After an anxious wait of almost a minute, he decided he'd not awakened anyone. He put two sandwiches and an apple in a brown paper bag for himself and three sandwiches and two apples in a bag for Sam. He was about to creep back along the dark hallway, to drag Sam out of bed, if necessary, when Sam appeared, bedroll under his arm. He, too, had chosen his blue *U.C. — Berkeley* sweat shirt. Seeing Allan's fishing gear, Sam started to return for his own, but Allan convinced him that one pole would be plenty.

They carried their bedrolls and lunch bags and fishing pole outside, opening and closing the various doors and gates with care. They stuffed their lunches inside their bedrolls and strapped the bedrolls on the metal carriers. Though it was chilly enough to wear his sweater, Allan decided to tie it around his throat and let it hang down his back the way the men at Berkeley wore their sweaters.

An inch or two of sun had edged above the horizon when they pushed their bikes out of the yard, settled onto their seats, and moved down the black asphalt road.

As Allan pedaled far ahead . . . he would try to go slow, so Sam could keep up with him . . . he glanced back. He had to swallow hard to keep the tears from popping into his eyes. It had to be wrong to feel so happy about leaving home. But no denying it: he was happy. He wanted to sing, but he'd better not. Not yet. He slowed down, so Sam could catch up with him, so he could communicate his happiness to Sam. Taking a keep breath, he inhaled the scent of the wet fields and the dew-drenched trees. Bending low over the handlebars, he heard the hum of the tires on the wet asphalt. He bent lower. The skin across his face and down his neck tingled at the prospects of adventure that lay ahead.

Maybe, he thought, maybe he should have returned his father's embrace last night.

He looked back once and did not look back again.

26

Chapter 2

The contents of every truck and trailer that used the Redwood County Dump was hastily but shrewdly appraised by Horace Butright.

When he'd accepted the job as Dump Attendant in 1911, all the trash was delivered in horse-drawn wagons. In 1960, after he'd fallen into the bed of a truck filled with plaster and lath, Horace built a tower fourteen feet high just inside the fence near the gate. A ladder reached to a deck at the top of the tower where, under a bright yellow beach umbrella, Horace sat in a tattered wicker armchair and directed the drivers with the authority of a general placing his troops.

Only inflammable material went to Section A. Section B received household trash (bottles, cans, boxes, barrels). Section C was restricted to timber and cuttings from trees, hedges, and lawns. Debris from the demolition of buildings went into Section D. From sunrise to long after sunset swarms of clattering gulls pecked away at the garbage in Section E, the corner of the dump most distant from the building Horace lived in. While hundreds of gulls gobbled up the most recent deposits, hundreds of other impatient gulls circled and dipped overhead, screaming for their share of the feast.

At the end of each day, after the gates were closed and locked, after the last truck and trailer had disappeared, Horace rushed to Section F, an area of approximately three acres separated from the building in which he lived by a fence of logs three times the thickness of telephone poles. There he picked and hammered and shoveled through the day's collection of tables and cabinets and stoves and chairs, through the books and newspapers, through the trunks and boxes and barrels that could conceal one more precious memento of a very precious past.

Thanks to the delivery of electricity in 1952, Horace could now work in the glow of bright spotlights strung on long extension wires from the house. Before, when he had no electricity, if he felt that some bright treasure lay waiting beneath the trash, he drove his Ford truck up to Section F and turned on the headlights. But now it was more difficult to find a source for the headlight bulbs. He'd long ago depleted his store, and not even the friendlier truck drivers, who, now and then, used to present him with the gift of a bulb or two . . . not even the friendlier truck drivers could locate one more bulb.

Now not just the bulbs were gone, but so was the battery. Or almost gone.

The last battery in existence had been unearthed here in Section F three years before. Horace had nursed it along as he might a loved and ailing child. If the battery survived another five or six hours, he would consider himself lucky. For some unexplainable reason the motor, unlike the transmission and the brake, continued to function well enough to at least put the truck in motion.

So, when the county supervisors had sanctioned the

28

stringing of wires from the highway to the dump, Horace, anxious to retire the loyal old Ford, had agreed. His embarrassment and guilt at betraying a code he'd laid down for himself forty years ago died a hard death. But a refrigerator, lights, a radio . . . they were not just luxuries. They sustained him. Once the wires were available, and the lights, he could, if he wished, work until midnight. He often did.

Many nights he had worked from the moment the last truck departed and he had locked the gates until he could no longer balance a shovel or swing a pick. Dredging up one last wisp of strength, he'd managed to drag his booty into the house, where it was cleaned, evaluated, and then stored on one of a thousand wooden shelves or one of several dozen tabletops or in the depths of one of the countless barrels, bags, or boxes. Or discarded. After gulping down a cheese or a salami sandwich and a cup of tea, he'd fallen into bed, to rise again at dawn to work the mound again in Section F before the arrival of that day's trucks.

Today, Sunday, there would be no trucks. He'd be able to spend the entire morning, as he did every Sunday, digging with pick and shovel and sometimes spoon or penknife. Then, after lunch, he could remain inside, at the workbench. Rain or shine, hot or cold, Sunday was the one day he lived for.

While he ate his fried eggs and toast, he thought about the difficulties he would have replenishing his stores after that old Ford gave up. Maybe he'd have to try powdered eggs again. He'd tried them once, during the war, but after one taste he'd offered the rest to the dozens of cats that prowled the dump. Fatty, his favorite, an orange tom with more scars than fur on his body, proved his superior wisdom. He was the only one of all the cats who, instead of eating the mess, turned his stiff tail to the plate and sprayed its contents.

29

He'd miss that old Ford. It had been more loyal to him than he had been to it. But why try to force it beyond its capacities? Two weeks ago, the last time he'd gone to Anders Corners, it had been barely able to climb the few hills. Its brakes were so unreliable that he'd traveled the seven miles in low gear. If the Ford, crouching there on the other side of the fence, were able to dream now, its dreams would probably be those same dreams that plagued Horace these nights: dreams of shadows, of sunsets, dreams of a dark cavern spreading open like jaws to devour him.

Until recently the truck had rested under the redwood tree, at the corner of the fence that surrounded Section F, source of many of its transplanted organs. Stricken at the sight of it cringing there under the tree when he stepped outside each morning, Horace had moved the truck to the far side of the opposite fence so it would not appear, each morning, to plague his conscience. He knew it was waiting, suffering in silence on the other side of the fence, but at least it was out of sight.

Perhaps, he mused now, as he washed his breakfast dishes, perhaps the collapse of the truck would prove to be a blessing. Were it to remain reliable, he might, during moments of laziness, be tempted to travel to Anders Corners more frequently. Those seconds spent nursing the Ford, those minutes devoted to reassuring acquaintances in town about his health, those hours given to gossiping with the three or four old-timers who ruled the past from their bus-bench throne in front of Jan Long's Hardware Store . . . all that time should be dedicated to Section F or to the partially reconstructed treasures Section F had already yielded. Treasures that filled the house and the building attached to the house.

Under the redwood tree Horace stretched and then broke into a laugh as Fatty raced under the house, a gray rat squirming and kicking in his jaws. Horace waited a moment longer, to watch the gulls swoop and glide and to listen to their cries; then he walked along the fence to the entry to Section F, trying to subdue the swell of hope that came like a dutiful guest each Sunday morning.

The last few Sundays had not been too fruitful, but this morning the first strike came less than five minutes after he started poking about in Saturday's deposits. He kicked aside a few empty crates and exposed an old Singer sewing machine that was not worth salvaging. He'd already restored six of the first Singers ever sold. They were standing now in their stalls, on the balcony in the barn, waiting for a woman in black buttoned shoes to walk in and draw up a stool and set her taffeta in place and start the treadle rocking.

Horace checked out the machine very carefully, alert for gears or wires or bobbins that just might be valuable in case he ever decided to rebuild a seventh Singer. When he finally heaved the machine aside to get at the crushed dresser beneath, his eye caught an object he knew he ought to recognize. As he fingered it, he half closed his eyes. He saw himself, a child, standing in a barn, in the shadows of an oat bin, watching an aged cowboy struggle up out of his blankets. There had to be a connection between that aged cowboy and this object gripped between his fingers.

Horace shook himself and plucked himself out of 1890, or 1900, and forced himself back to 1970, to the Redwood County Dump, to Section F. He set the . . . whatever it was . . . aside. He'd take it back to the house where he'd examine it at his leisure and decide if it could or should be repaired. He was not anxious about his momentary failure to identify it. In his own good time he'd remember, he'd thumb through a catalogue or two for a few details he might have forgotten, and he would print the brief description on a card. And almost cer-

31

tainly, sooner or later, in or out of his dreams, the form and face of that aged cowboy would fight its way over the trails of the past to today.

In the next forty minutes Horace found two more objects, one of which he recognized immediately. He rushed back to the house and into the barn, to sit at his workbench.

The first of the three discoveries was made of leather and smeared with a thick green mold. What had once been elastic side straps were almost totally rotted away. As he turned it over and over in his hands, Horace traveled back over those ancient trails, into the shadow of the barn, where he watched the old cowboy bring himself, with great grunting efforts, erect. With tender manipulation of his hands and a delicate tilt to his body, the cowboy slipped a device inside his long underwear, around his waist, over his lower abdomen. He tightened the straps and buttoned his underwear and, with one long sigh of relief, he straightened his body. Horace clapped his hands together and, humming to himself, cleaned the leather with a brush and soapy water. He wiped it dry and rubbed it with Neatsfoot oil. From a small tin box (labeled *Elastic, All Kinds, All Sizes*) he removed the appropriate strips and fed them through the openings in the leather. In a ship's trunk (labeled *Rubber Tubing*) he found the piece of tubing of the precise diameter required. Satisfied, finally, that the finished product looked just as it had looked when it had first been used seventy or eighty or ninety years ago, Horace removed a three by five card from the stack ever present on the corner of his workbench.

Grinning with pride and satisfaction at the facility with which his mind still functioned (even as his memory continued to work, continued to retrieve the creased bronze features of the face of that cowboy now long buried and turned to dust), he printed the words that some day . . . long after he, Horace, was dead and buried and turned to dust . . . the words that some day would identify this strange object to whoever might be gazing at it, might be wondering what purpose the device had served.

Standing, he examined a bookshelf suspended above his workbench. Filling a stretch of at least six feet was a tightly packed assortment of magazines, catalogues, and folders filled with select ads out of newspapers from Butte, Montana, and Abilene, Kansas, and Chicago and New York and San Francisco. In most of the newspaper ads the copy was faded and worn from age and use; in some of the magazines and catalogues the pages were covered with a patina of grime so thick that the relevant information could not be read. But always, eventually, he discovered the information he needed. This morning he found it on page 64 of Boyer's Catalogue, published in Boston in 1900.

With a faintly quivering hand he printed, on one of the three by five cards stacked on his bench, the information he felt was important. He fixed the card with twine to the beltlike object he'd successfully restored. Finished, he held it at arm's length to review his accomplishment.

ABDOMINAL SUPPORTER
1. Morrocco Leather
2. Passary, held in position by tubes
3. Approx. Cost...$2.75

After examining the second object he'd unearthed in Section F, Horace decided to set it aside and return to it later. A more conscientious probing of his memories than he was yet prepared for would be required for that one, a ruthless dash through the past, smashing through the obstacles demanding more immediate, more intimate attention.

"Come back to it," Horace murmured. "Later."

The third object had been fixed by decades of dust and water to the inner wall of a dented brass box, which, in turn, was almost lost inside a battered, unreclaimable leather satchel. Not a moment's doubt about this, a comb of black rubber embossed on one side with the figure of a trotting horse.

Horace washed the comb in kerosene, and he scrubbed it with a stiff bristle brush. No need for the catalogues for this.

BLACK RUBBER COMB
for Horse's Mane

Approx. Cost ... 13$

He tied the twine to the comb and he laid it aside. Now, with a faint twinge of excitement . . . was it fear? . . . Horace returned to the final object to be identified.

It was, obviously, a crank.

A crank.

Where, among the hundreds of treasures still not totally reconstructed . . . treasures that required a crank . . . where would such a crank (a crank with a tip so strangely fluted) fit? What sort of shaft would such a crank have been designed to rotate? And rotate for what purpose?

Horace left his bench and went through the doorway into the house. He'd eat some lunch and then, with food in his stomach, he'd be able to think more clearly. When he opened the cupboard in which he stored his canned goods, his eye was jolted by a label on a can: an ear of corn dropping golden kernels into a white bowl.

34

Twelve steps took him from the cupboard and back through the door of the barn to his workbench. A switch at the side of the bench lit three lights strung along the central roof beam.

Horace scurried down the aisle between the stacks of cartons and barrels (all labeled with the same fine spider-web printing). He climbed the stairs at the far end of the barn to the balcony that was supported, it seemed, by not much more than a wish. Narrow stalls filled the north wall of the balcony from floor to ceiling. Identification cards hung from the ceiling at the entry to each stall. Horace entered the stall containing

FARM EQUIPMENT, SMALL

The interior of the stall, like all the other stalls, was filled with rows of bins, which, in turn, were filled with boxes or burlap bags or wooden crates or kegs, all of them fitted with their own identification cards. On the side of the crate Horace now withdrew were the words, printed in the same spidery hand, Corn Sheller.
He carried the crate along the balcony and down the stairs and up the aisle to his workbench. He lit the lamp over the bench, the lamp he'd constructed from dozens of parts plucked from dozens of Luxor lamps that had found their way to the dump the past few years. Like the electricity and then the refrigerator, the lamp was one of the few concessions Horace had made to contemporary domestic luxury. It really wasn't a luxury, he'd reasoned, if it helped preserve his eyesight so he might continue his work.

Horace eased the crank into the aperture of the shaft. The shaft revolved, grudgingly. He removed the crank, dismantled the machine, cleaned each piece in kerosene and then in oil, and carefully fit the pieces together.

He turned the crank. Better, but still not as smooth

35

as it should be. He took it apart and examined each piece under a magnifying glass (fixed to the end of a carved ivory handle and enclosed within an elliptical silver frame, the empty sockets of which had once held precious stones). The teeth of one gear had tiny burrs, and, in addition, the face of a second gear was coated with flakes of rust. With a file the size of a toothpick he smoothed the burrs on the teeth, and then, with fine emery cloth, he buffed the rusty gear-face. After he wiped and oiled each piece, he fitted them all together again. Perfect!

Horace leaned back. In the last year or so, after such fierce concentration, he'd often found himself so exhausted that he'd had to close his eyes and just sit there, resting. He was that exhausted now.

His half-closed eyes created a blurred halo about the border of the corn sheller, that strange assemblage of wood and gears that was as much a part of his past, his childhood, as his mother or his father. Even more . . . even more. He had . . . with great effort, true . . . but he had recognized it, he had identified it.

How long had it been since he'd first started work on that corn sheller? Ten years at least. And here it was . . . now . . . in 1970 . . . completed. Completed and now to be stored among the thousands of other artifacts he . . . *he,* Horace Butright . . . had saved from extinction.

And those thousands of three by five cards . . . those thousands of words he'd printed. At first the line had been firm and fine, his energy unlimited. There had been days then when he'd completed six or seven pieces a day. At night, after checking catalogues or magazines or old newspapers, he'd printed the cards and fixed them with twine. Now and then, with a twinge of pain, when he came upon an old card, one he'd printed when he'd only been here a year or so, he could not help but notice how firm and fine the line of his print had been. Often now there would be five or six days without a discovery, without the printing of a card.

As the years had rushed after each other, his various discoveries had crowded out his table and then his bed and his sink and his stove. He'd had to build another building to house the overflow and then a balcony in the barnlike structure and then cubbies and closets on the balcony.

The cards played cruel games with his memory. Events that had retreated into extinction would, with the sight of a certain wheel or strap or lever, with the touch of a certain texture, with the certain scent of a soap or powder or an oil or a paint or a flower, those ancient events would rush forward through the canyons of the past, revived, in too extreme detail, stirring other memories, old and new, struggling to swell his throat with laughter or wring his heart and fill his eyes with tears. Were they true, those memories? Had those events occurred? Were they real or fantasy?

Horace wiped his face with his oily hands, tried to stand, but gave up and sat again. He closed his eyes. Ah yes, there they were, stealing toward him through the haze of his exhaustion, absolutely refusing anymore to be diverted . . . *the slow advance down the rows between the cornstalks, the pull and rip of each ear, the pungent aroma of sun-browned cornsilk, and then, in the cool shade of the silo, the shucking and shelling . . . and oh, the ache low in his back.*

Or was the ache he thought he was recalling really the ache that at this very moment, at his workbench, stiffened his spine and burned his shoulders?

There, on the bench, lay the card, completed. For a moment he wondered who could have written the words. Who, indeed, could have counterfeited that writing? He

37

read the title at the top of the card aloud. "Corn Sheller."
And then, in the shade of the silo, the shucking and shelling . . . and oh, the ache . . .

CORN SHELLER

1. Mounted on box
2. Separates corn from cob
3. Deposits corn in box on which it is mounted and deposits cob outside.
4. Will shell all ears, size no difference.
5. Approx. Cost . . .

He'd not printed the price. Well, that could be written later. He did not want to reinforce the power of his memory. He wanted to evade that memory now, escape it, survive it.

He left the workbench and walked through the house and out the front door, to stand again under the redwood tree. What was happening? Was his mind, like that dilapidated Ford truck, disintegrating? Turning to dust inside his skull before his body was even buried? He'd had the strength, until now, to restrain his memories, or at least control them, or at least not permit them to disturb him.

Horace glanced down at his hands. They were trembling. His face was wet.

What was happening? He'd had such grand hopes for this day, but now . . . now those hopes were being challenged, were being threatened.

He looked up into the redwood tree. Nothing there

38

to give him comfort. He watched the gulls swarm over the garbage. Usually their screams reassured him, but they gave him no reassurance this morning. He might just as well be the only living creature at the dump.

Maybe if he returned to the bench, if he worked, really *worked* . . . maybe that would help.

Back at the bench, he picked up the comb, on which he'd already worked. There was the card, completed, tied securely. He considered a few bits and pieces of cloth. Dresses for babies, the cloth decomposed. They'd not last another year. No use wasting time or space. He dropped them into a box containing material to be discarded.

He returned to the kitchen, stood about for a moment trying to decide why he'd come there. Well, since he was there, he may as well eat. He made a peanut butter sandwich and drank a glass of chilled apple juice. After he stacked the dishes in the sink, he stepped outside. In the shade of the redwood he felt stronger, more content.

The day, once again, swelled with promise.

As he hurried along the fence to the entry of Section F, he had the eerie feeling he was being watched. He turned his head. There were two boys sitting on bicycles just outside the locked gates.

One of the boys, about to rush away, was trying to urge his friend to leave with him. But the friend, leaning against the link fence, pressing his face against the wire, waved at Horace.

Chapter 3

It was like those mornings at camp when he'd slipped out of his bedroll and left his tent to stand in the wet black moonlight, almost tasting the scent of pine and cypress. Now the air was filled with the pungent camphor scent from the eucalyptus trees closed into an arch above the road.

Sam bent over the handlebars. He liked the sound the tires made on the dew-drenched asphalt. He raised his head to locate the birds beginning to stir in the leaves, calling to each other through the foggy dawn. A rabbit hopped out of the grass beyond the fence at the side of the road. It stopped, sat up, twitched its nose, heard and then saw Sam, and left a puff of gravel behind as it darted back under the fence to the security of the tall grass.

Far down the road, almost out of sight, Allan's blue sweat shirt reminded Sam that Allan was keeping his word. He was not rushing ahead, not trying to leave Sam behind.

Sam stretched his shoulders and tilted back his head.

40

Just think: he had almost refused Allan's suggestion that they run away. Now he was sorry they'd waited as long as they had.

Somewhere out beyond the trees, far back from the road, a crow gave three hoarse coughs. From the grass near the fence, a meadowlark's song shamed the crow into silence. Sam tried to duplicate the song of the lark, but no matter how he shaped his lips or rolled his tongue, every note had the same thin tone. He imitated the crow so successfully that one crow dipped down out of the trees to inspect him. Complaining twice at its having been duped, it returned to the trees.

With a rush, in one instant, all the birds in all the trees were awake, darting from tree to tree, filling the air with song. A covey of quail, exploring the weeds at the side of the road, announced his approach with a chorus of alarmed whistles and scurried under the fence to the safety of the grass.

Sam aimed a gun composed of a thumb and forefinger at a pair of hawks drifting overhead on the early autumn currents. He fired twice . . . "Pi-koo! Pi-koo!" . . . but the hawks continued their solemn circular glides.

Sheep, bedded beneath the grotesque live oaks and squat, solid laurels, rose to their feet to observe Sam's approach. A few, closest to the fence, trotted off, twitching their stubby tails. Four Black Angus heifers pondered the gun aimed now in their direction and continued chewing their cuds as each in turn was mercilessly and unsuccessfully executed. "Pi-koo! Pi-koo! Pi-koo! Pi-koo!"

Leaning first right and then left, Sam weaved his bike from one edge of the road to the other. Then, his feet on the handlebars and his arms stretched out, he lay back, resting his head on the bedroll strapped in the basket on the rear fender. Now a daredevil rider with Ringling Brothers Circus, he guided his bike without watching the road. Sam was not famous among his friends for such daring, and he wondered now, as the eucalyptus branches rushed by overhead and the bright morning sun twinkled through the quivering leaves, why he always let Allan be the hero. When he straightened up, he felt he'd accomplished something much more satisfying than gluing pieces of balsawood together. If he went to the circus tonight, he'd not sink his head in Thelma's lap when the Flying Palumbos sailed through the air.

Ralph, that night, had also hidden his eyes, as had Rebecca. But Allan hadn't.

His mother and father had planned and promised to take him and Allan, but at the last moment they'd discovered they had to go to a dinner in San Francisco. They'd called Thelma. Would she be willing to take the boys? They'd pay for tickets for her children, too, of course. And they'd pay for food and taxis and whatever other expenses there would be. They'd made a promise to the boys, and, Mrs. Collins had told Thelma, promises to children ought to be kept.

Sam had sat next to Thelma. Rebecca had sat on the other side. Then Ralph and Allan.

When the trainer fought off the tigers, Sam and Rebecca had clutched Thelma's hands. She'd tried to reassure them, insisting that the tiger had been trained to roar and claw and charge at the trainer that way. When the Flying Palumbos had somersaulted through the air, catching at wrists or ankles or iron bars at the very last moment, Sam and Rebecca had pressed their heads into Thelma's lap. She'd laughed and assured them that when the Palumbos were safe and the act had been completed, she'd let them know so they could raise their heads and see the clowns in the crazy car.

They'd stayed at Thelma's house that night, the four children sleeping in one room. When Thelma had come in to turn off the light and had kissed them all good night, Allan had asked if he and Sam could always live there

42

with Becky and Ralph. Thelma had said that she didn't think Mr. and Mrs. Collins would go for that, and anyway, if they lived with her all the time, they wouldn't think she was so special. They'd want to go back to Orchid to live with their own momma and poppa. "We live here all the time," Rebecca had said, "and we think you're special." Thelma had given Rebecca an extra kiss and said, well, there were lots of reasons Sam and Allan couldn't stay there in Oakland and, anyway, it was late and they'd better go to sleep. After she'd closed the door, they'd had a contest to see who could stay awake the longest. Sam won, but of course no one was awake to witness his victory, so the next day they didn't believe him.

When Thelma went to work the next morning, Sam and Allan said good-bye to Rebecca and Ralph and rode on the bus with Thelma from Oakland to Orchid.

Had that been the last time they'd stayed at Thelma's house? Sam tried now to remember more recent visits. No, that had been the last time. He'd been what . . . six? seven? A long time ago.

Sam bowed out his legs to fit the barrel body of his palomino that had carried him out of reach of the posse that had been chasing ("tailing," Allan would say) him and Allan for a week. They'd robbed a Wells-Fargo bank and had distributed most of the money among poor ranchers about to have their land taken by the bank. They'd saved a small portion of money so they might buy more horses and fancy boots and wide leather belts with brass rivets.

"Hey, Sam. Come on."

Allan was waving, pointing at a break in the fence. Before Sam reached him, Allan had left the road and was through the fence and on his way across the meadow.

Being the leader, Allan could go where he wished. Once, when they'd left a good road to push their bikes across a creek and up a grass-covered hill, Allan had explained that their parents would be put off this way, they'd not be able to set any *tail* on them.

Sam warmed in the sense of his own sophistication. He did not have to ask what *tail* meant. Allan and his friends might think him young and timid, but secretly he was convinced that, thanks to the instructive TV and Saturday night movies, he could probably fight his way through any street or alley of the underworld.

Sam chased after his brother, scattering sheep and even persuading the stubborn cattle to respect his power. For the next hour they pushed their bikes through waist-high grass, rode down roads barely wide enough for a single car, lifted their bikes over and dragged them under fences, portaged them across creeks that, in another month, would be rivers. And always, according to Allan, always moving north.

Sam never understood Allan when he'd explained, at camp, how to locate north once you knew the sun always moved from east to west. What happened on those days when there was no sun? And what about nighttime? What if you wanted to know what direction you were going at midnight? And what if you just couldn't remember that the sun rose in the east and set in the west and you sometimes reversed it? If you had the sun rising in the west, you were lost. Sam could only hope that in the two years before he'd be as old as Allan was now, he'd be as good as Allan at things like finding what direction north lay, knowing the tricks that kept you from being tailed, and never losing your cool when doing exactly what your mother or father had just warned you not to do.

They stopped to eat their sandwiches on a cliff above a lake gleaming black in the shadows of the hills and trees. Flocks of geese skimmed the water, settled, rose, and settled again.

Sam's sides were still heaving, and sweat continued to roll down his cheeks and his neck while he ate. For the last ten minutes he'd been pumping his bike as fast as he could in an unsuccessful effort to catch Allan, to persuade him to stop for lunch. He'd worn his sweat shirt when he'd left the house, but now it was draped over his shoulders, the way Allan wore his.

Allan opened the bottle of cider they'd bought at a roadside stand (along with a box of karmelcorn), and, after drinking, he offered the bottle to Sam.

Sam ate his three sandwiches in the time it took Allan to eat his two. Before returning the jug to Allan, Sam drank almost half of the cider. He lay on his back, his arms over his eyes. He wiped his flushed face with the sleeve of his sweat shirt. "How far do you think we've gone, Al?"

"Oh, twenty miles. Maybe thirty."

Sam rolled onto his side to take another swallow of cider. Then Allan drank the rest.

"I can see Orchid," Sam said, shading his eyes with his right hand. He could not, but he could see the dip in the hills beyond which, he was sure, Lafayette and Orinda and Walnut Creek must lie and, beyond them, Orchid. "You think they know we're gone yet?" Sam asked, picking a piece of nonexistent dust from a piece of karmelcorn.

"Nah," Allan said. "We've been gone this long before."

"Not on Sundays. This time on Sundays we're always at church. By now they've been in to wake us up. They know we're gone."

"When we don't show up for lunch, that's when they'll start to wonder."

"What do you think they'll do, Al?"

"Like I said, they'll probably call the cops."

"You really think they will?"

"Sure."

"Maybe they'll think . . . you know . . . maybe they'll think we're kidnapped or something. Dad's sort of rich. Maybe they'll think we've been kidnapped and we're being held for ransom."

"You think kidnappers would let us take our bikes with us?"

Being older and being two grades ahead of Sam and having read so many more detective stories, it was natural that Allan would have the talent for resolving such complicated problems. The very talent, according to his father, that helped explain Allan's cynicism.

That was what his father had said the evening Allan had refused to stop reading and help set up the Ping-Pong table.

His father had mumbled something about how he was getting damn tired of Allan's sitting around, letting other people work, and then enjoying himself after the work was done. Allan had said, well, since he'd not be playing Ping-Pong, would that make his sitting around OK?

"You're too damn young to be so arrogant," his father had said. "Where the hell are you learning to be so arrogant? That's what I'd like to know."

Sam always envied Allan his ability to sense that point beyond which his father's anger would erupt. It had almost, but not quite, been at that point then.

Allan had continued reading until he'd completed the page. Then, casually, he'd leafed through four or five pages to see how much of the chapter remained. He'd put down the book and stood up to help. His father had pushed him back into the chair. "I don't need your help now. Sam and I can do it. But just you remember. Don't you so much as bounce a ball on this table."

Allan, unruffled, had picked up his reading where

he'd left off. For a moment Sam had thought his father would rip the book out of Allan's hands. Instead, he'd shaken his head and, mumbling, he'd gone into the house. From the kitchen Sam could hear his mother's reassurance that this nastiness was just a phase all boys go through. Sam would go through it, too, when he was older.

"We should have left a note," Sam said. "Not for Dad so much. He can take it. But Mom . . ."

"I did leave a note."

Allan never lied. Well, almost never. When he did, it was never a big or serious lie. Why should he think Allan was lying now?

"I wrote it while you were getting dressed."

"You did? Honest?"

"Yeah. I left it on the kitchen table."

"I didn't see it."

"Did you look for it?"

"Well, no."

"Then of course you didn't see it. I left it beside the toaster."

"What did you say?"

Allan stood up. He leaned back and threw the empty cider jug. It cast fragments of sunlight spinning free as it dropped, as it flipped over and over until, finally, it was lost in the sand and rocks below.

"I said, 'Dear Mom and Dad, me and Sam have gone off on a ride. We'll be gone for a while, probably for a long time. Don't worry because we can take care of ourselves. Sincerely, Allan and Sam.'"

Satisfied, Sam jumped onto his bike and followed Allan down the road.

To avoid the steep and winding hill that promised to grow steeper and even more winding, they climbed a rail fence and walked their bikes through tall brown rye-

47

grass. They reached a rutted road, and Allan stopped to check the sun. He nodded at his shadow and pointed. "That way's north."

The edges of occasional puddles were trimmed with tire marks. Since Allan had chosen the left lane, Sam accepted the right, alert for potholes and rocks that could wrench the handlebars out of his fingers and toss him into the ditch.

After crossing two creeks and another fence, they found themselves on an asphalt road, smoother and more level than the one before. Sam tried to ignore the tears the cold wind brought to his eyes, and he tried to pedal faster so he might keep up with Allan, but no matter how hard he tried, the distance between them grew greater. Finally, because of the tears and the distance, he could no longer distinguish Allan's blue sweat shirt.

Sam relaxed. His legs were beginning to tire. If he were home, he would have eaten three times as much food as he'd eaten so far today. What would he eat tonight? And where would he eat? And tomorrow? And the next day?

What would they do after they spent their money?

Sam stopped pedaling as he approached a bend in the road. A sign showed a sharply angled arrow and, black on yellow, the words *Slow to 20 m.p.h.*

Sam rounded the bend and there, on its side, in the dirt alongside the road, lay Allan's bike. Was Allan sprawled somewhere in the brush, his leg broken, unconscious? "Allan! Where are you? Hey, Allan!"

"I'm up here."

The boulder was as large as their house in Orchid. Sitting on top, his arms around his knees, Allan was staring off into space.

Several minutes and two bruised shins later, Sam settled his tired body beside Allan's.

To the west, beyond the green hills, lay the ocean.

48

To the east the freeway, alive with an army of ants, stretched out to the Golden Gate Bridge and beyond, to the city of San Francisco pinned to the hills by the sunlight.

Allan indicated a large truck that had parked on the shoulder of the freeway. Could Sam guess the number of cars that passed the truck in sixty seconds? Allan would count the cars going one way and Sam would count them going the other. They guessed . . . Sam saying four hundred and Allan saying six hundred . . . and they started counting. When Sam had reached two hundred and twenty-three, Allan lay back. "No use," he said, "we don't have a watch. We don't know when it's been sixty seconds."

"How far were you?"

"Three seventeen."

"I was at two twenty-three," Sam said. How far, he asked Allan, did he think it was to the ocean? How far to the bridge? To the city? How many miles had they gone that day so far? How many more would they go? And then Sam asked if maybe they ought to try to find a store so they could buy something to eat. "A sandwich or a candy bar," he said. "I'd sure like a thick ham sandwich and a Baby Ruth bar. Yum."

Allan had little interest in food. "How many times do you guess we've gone down that freeway and crossed the bridge?"

Sam said maybe twenty and Allan said no, it had been lots more than twenty, and Sam said again that he was hungry and they ought to look for a store. Allan said that if they were home, they'd be crossing the Richmond Bridge today because their father was going to take them to Bolinas.

"And then something special," Sam said. "Some new big project. The biggest job he's ever had. I'm hungry."

"What's that?" Allan said, standing and shielding his eyes with both hands.

Allan, Sam knew, was simply trying to distract him. He did not even bother to stand.

"I wonder what it is," Allan said.

"I'm hungry. And you didn't keep your promise."

"What promise?"

"You know what promise."

"I didn't run away. I only got a little ahead. I always came back, didn't I? I wonder what that is."

Sam gave in. "OK, what *what* is?"

"That cloud."

"It's a cloud," Sam said. On the far side of the freeway, to the north, a few miles inland from the ocean, a gray cloud rose and fell, changing shape even as they watched.

Sam was torn between hunger and homesickness. If he were home now, he'd be sitting at the snackbar in the kitchen, eating a bowl of ice cream or a milkshake, either of which he might never eat again. Would there be ice cream wherever they were going? With great reluctance he let his anger succumb to his own growing curiosity about the strange cloud. "What is it, Al? It's weird."

"Let's go see." And before Sam could announce his reluctance, Allan had descended the boulder and was racing down the road. By the time Sam reached his bike, Allan was out of sight.

They continued on the asphalt road, with Allan always directing them toward the cloud, which was lost from sight at times as it fell behind clumps of trees and intervening hills. Then, abruptly, there it would be, rolling and tumbling and changing shape.

More fences . . . more creeks . . . more narrow roads. Before they could change their direction, they went riding up one slope and speeding down another

50

onto a four-lane highway. Cars rushed past, the drivers honking their horns. A bald man, his florid face almost filling the window space of his Porsche, shouted, "Get off the highway, you idiots! Get off the highway!"

Riding as close to the shoulder as he dared, Sam kept shouting to Allan that they weren't allowed to ride on freeways, that they'd been warned by both their mother and their father that it was a crime . . . they'd go to jail . . . they had to get off the highway. Sam, with one terrified glance, looked down on the freeway beneath them. All the cars in the world seemed to be hurtling themselves directly at him. A driver behind him pounded on his horn. Several drivers, passing him, shouted curses or threats. When Allan chose the first exit, Sam, with great relief, glided down the incline behind him.

Across the overpass, finally, they were once again on a blacktop road. The cloud had settled behind a hill. But Sam had lost interest in the cloud. He was more concerned at the moment about the odor. If it didn't fade, he was going to be sick.

"Something must have died around here," Sam called, but Allan, far ahead, did not hear him or did not choose to reply.

The odor grew stronger. Sam, who often found it great fun to make jokes about topics that might disgust his classmates while they ate their lunch, now discovered his own stomach to be weaker than he would have believed.

Allan seemed unaffected by the odor. He'd stopped and was leaning on his bike, waiting for Sam to catch up.

"Wow," Sam said. "What's that stink?"

"Don't you remember? When we drive to the ocean we smell it."

"Yeah, but never this strong. What is it?"

"The garbage dump."

"Ugh! Let's not go any closer."

Was Allan really not bothered by it or was he putting on a show for Sam's benefit? He was good at pretending. Sometimes his defiance at home seemed to Sam to be a performance for Sam's appreciation. Was he a traitor when he failed to respond to such defiance? When he saw the dismay on his father's or mother's face, he wanted to assure them that Allan was just pretending; they need have no fear. Fear of what, he wasn't sure.

"You'll get used to it," Allan said. "Anyway, I bet the dump's a cool place. People throw all kinds of things away at dumps. We might find something important."

With that remark, before Sam could call out his disapproval, Allan rode off again. Sam, swallowing hard, mounted his Schwinn and forced himself to follow. He hated to admit it, but once again Allan was correct. As the odor grew stronger, it also grew less nauseating. Either that or, as Allan had promised, he was growing used to it.

Sam saw Allan's bike speed up a short incline and over the top and out of sight. He pumped hard, and then he, too, sailed up and . . . before he moved beyond the crest and down the hill . . . he saw the cloud. And he knew why the cloud had seemed to be changing shape.

Thousands of sea gulls were flying around a flat plain at the bottom of the hill Sam was now descending. The birds rose and fell, constantly altering the shape of their mass, with a few derelict gulls moving off alone and a few new arrivals moving in to take their places. Maybe, Sam thought, the dump would prove a relief. He had to admit, his bottom was beginning to ache. They'd be able to walk at the dump, able to rest their legs. One thing for sure he'd not be able to do was *eat*. Even the thought of food made his stomach shiver.

Allan turned at the intersection of the asphalt road and a dirt road, and Sam, arriving at the intersection a few minutes later, noticed a piece of splintered plywood nailed to a post. At the top of the plywood someone had painted a shaky red arrow that pointed down the dirt road Allan had taken. Under the arrow, in a black script as trembly as the arrow, were two words: Counry Dump.

The appearance of the land had changed. Until now they'd been moving through meadows covered with rye-grass and wild buckwheat as high as their hips and groves of eucalyptus and cottonwood and twisted California oaks, but now, on either side of the road, there was nothing but brown sand and dry mud. Swirls of sand, whipped by the wind, moved across the ground. It was plain, even to Sam (who'd never read the detective stories Allan had read and who had no pretensions to solving some day an international spy mystery) that the land had recently been scraped by a tractor. The tread marks of huge tires had hardened in the mud, and the shining scrape marks of the blade were still visible at the side of the road that dipped between the two banks and turned to slope down again. Sam braked his bike, not sure what might be waiting for him. Once around the bend, he released the hand brakes. Allan was standing in the middle of the road, leaning on his bike, waiting, studying the high iron link fence ahead. Behind closed and locked gates the road continued across the dry mud flat to a tall redwood tree rising above what Sam thought at first to be a pile of debris. Moving closer, he recognized the debris to be shaped somewhat like two buildings, one small, like an ancient cottage, and another one, larger, shaped like a barn. The barn behind the cottage rose above it and leaned forward, to rest, or support itself, on the cottage roof.

Fifty yards or so from the house, if indeed it was a house, a tractor leaned back on its tail, its inclined blade hovering over the lip of a ravine into which it had pushed . . . yesterday, perhaps even today . . . a mound of shrubs and grass cuttings.

The wind, sweeping dust clouds across the expanse of trash and garbage, carried the calls of the gulls as they picked at the mounds or hovered over a bit of clear space that must have promised a rare delicacy.

"Let's go back, Allan. This place looks haunted."

Allan might have agreed had a man not appeared just then from the smaller of the two buildings. A black baseball cap, with the orange emblem of the San Francisco Giants clearly visible, was pushed far back on his head. As he walked toward the tractor, he reached up and pulled the cap forward, fixing the peak low over his eyes. Then he turned. He gazed at the boys for a moment, as if he were having a difficult time focusing on them.

"Let's go back," Sam said, swinging his bike around and climbing onto the seat.

"Come on," Allan said. He mounted his bike and let it coast down the road. Sam hated him at that moment. He would have turned around and returned home, but he knew that he'd never find his way. Why had he come? Why had he let Allan convince him his mother and father were evil?

Well, Allan hadn't really said they were *evil*. And Sam hadn't needed much convincing.

Reluctantly, Sam coasted along behind Allan toward the gate.

Chapter 4

Had it been any day but Sunday and any Sunday but this Sunday, Horace would have ignored the boys. Wanderers and curiosity-seekers often came to the gate on weekends and tried to convince him to let them in. He never did. Now and then, at night, some young man bent on impressing his girl friend would drive up to the gate and flick his lights off and on and blow his horn and shout obscenities or what he considered witty threats.

Horace, unimpressed, would continue his work at the bench.

Last summer, just a week or so after the Fourth of July, a carload of young men determined to accomplish more than threats had actually managed to climb the fence. Their mistake had been to enlighten Horace about their intentions as they approached the house.

A few hours before dark that day Horace had recovered a large store of fireworks from Section F. Four rockets and three Roman candles aimed in the direction of the invaders put them and their car to a hasty and fiery retreat.

Since that night he'd not been bothered. But he took no chance. Just inside the front door, in a wooden barrel, the remainder of the rockets and the Roman candles were stored in ready reserve.

Officially, the dump was open on Saturdays until noon, but the last straggler rarely left until one or two o'clock, which meant that Sunday was Horace's one full day of freedom. He would have refused to be diverted by two or two dozen young boys at the gate on a Sunday, but today was unlike other recent Sundays. His discoveries this morning had revived his spirit. The wheel had turned full cycle, and he was certain he was about to begin a whole new period of discovery. Goodwill warmed his tired old bones, overflowed, and insisted it be shared with another human being. Not Fatty, not the noisy gulls, or the inanimate redwood tree, but something human. Like a young boy. Or like two young boys.

It was about time he shed his despair, which he'd worn so long without relief that it had taken the shape of his soul, like a jacket worn every day, year after year, shapes itself to every eccentricity of the body it covers.

Yes, about time. Now, perhaps, he might awaken each morning, bright and alert, ready for work. As recently as yesterday he'd lain in his narrow bed, pretending that the alarm had not rung, considering the effort involved in resetting the alarm and sleeping for another fifteen or twenty minutes. He'd never done that before.

Every morning every year of his life, even on Sundays, the bell on his Beacon alarm clock had been choked into silence with the same flopping of arms and legs that had carried him out from under his blankets and across the floor to the toilet. This morning he'd lain there again, after he'd silenced the alarm, thinking that maybe, just maybe, if he stored up this extra bit of sleep just one time, he'd get the need for it out of his system.

Then, for some mysterious reason, what should he

56

think of but the visit last week, last Wednesday . . . or was it Thursday? . . . by that gang from the City Hall. He also recalled in complete detail their facetious (or were they facetious?) comments about his age. About his isolation. "What would you do if you had a heart attack, Butright? . . . Or pneumonia or something? . . . You know, you ain't no spring chicken, Butright. . . . You oughta retire and sit on a porch and (ha! ha!) watch the pretty girls go by." They were half his age, less than half his age. Where did they get off calling him *Butright,* as if he were their personal valet?

The visit and then the much too glib, much too ready-at-hand assurance that the visit meant nothing had, of course, made him suspect the opposite. The visit had meant something. The men were politicians, and politicians don't make visits to county dumps just to express concern for the health of the dump attendant. That visit had meant *some*thing. While they'd tramped over the dump, riding the tractor so they wouldn't mess their shoes in the mucky places, Horace had tried so hard to impress them with his stamina and efficiency that he was near collapse when they'd left. He'd closed and locked the gate an hour early. He'd fed Fatty and, without so much as a cup of tea for supper, he'd gone to bed and he'd lain there, in the darkness, shivering.

The rest of the week had proven no better than the first few fruitless days. Then this morning, in the space of one hour, he'd found the truss and the crank and the comb. Surely an omen to celebrate. In that spirit of celebration he decided to talk to the two boys at the fence.

Both boys, he noticed, carried packs on their backs. Expensive fishing gear in a canvas sack was roped to the frame of one bike. Two bored youngsters, Horace decided, out for some Sunday excitement. Bored and probably spoiled . . . nothing to do . . . slumming. Well, they were visitors, and in his time here he'd entertained precious few visitors. No one knew better than he did that he'd just about lost the knack of talking to people. Who now could be better to talk to than *boys?* Wasn't it boyhood he'd been celebrating the last fifty-eight years of his life?

Celebrating?

A strange word for his obsession of half a century. *Reviving* was a better word. Or, even better, *re-creating.* Wasn't it boyhood he was re-creating?

The two boys were younger than they'd appeared at first. He'd thought they were teen-agers, but the older of the two couldn't be much more than eleven. The younger was ten, perhaps nine.

Nine years old.

A long-forgotten, long-dead scene out of a Sunday of his own ninth year stirred itself alive, to become, in that instant, as real and as immediate as if that Sunday were this Sunday . . . *a summer Sunday morning thick with the hum of flies and bees . . . the two rocking chairs facing each other on the wide porch that clung to the house, not just across the front but around both sides, clear to the screen door leading into the kitchen . . .*

Of all his lifetime, of all his long lifetime of more than a thousand summer Sundays, why, now, *that* one?

. . . green head-high stalks of corn as far as the eye could see from the porch or even from the roof of the house . . . the aromas of summer fields on a summer Sunday . . . a dog behind the barn, at the edge of the pond . . .

Buster. The dog's name. All these years Buster had ceased to exist until now, today, this instant. Buster . . .

. . . barking, punishing frogs or snakes or fish or all three . . . the whinny of a lazy old mare named Lady

58

from the meadow . . . a Plymouth Rock rooster chasing a hen across the porch and up (with feathers and cackles flying) over the banister and down toward the pigpen . . . and the call, that call which he'd known all morning and all the night before would be coming, as inevitable as the coming of dusk or dawn: "Horse . . . Horse . . . where are you, Horse? . . . It's time to go, honey . . . Horse . . . hey, you, Horse . . . Horace Butright . . ."

"Hey, are you deaf?"

The older boy's head was cocked to the side, and he was squinting.

"Deaf? Me?" Horace heard a very faint echo of Lady's whinny and then, again, he said, "Deaf? Me? No, I'm not deaf. Why?"

"I asked if you lived here."

The younger boy whispered, "Let's go, Al. Come on."

"Yeah, I live here. You want to come in?"

"No," the younger one said. "We have to go."

"Well," the older one said, "is it all right?"

"Of course it's all right. I just invited you. And I'm the boss here."

"Maybe . . . could we just have a drink of water?"

"I'm not thirsty, Allan." The younger boy tugged at the older one's sleeve. "I think we oughta go."

"Aw," Horace said, "come on. I got plenty of water. I even got a refrigerator now I have electricity. So I've got ice, too." Horace removed the metal ring of keys from his coveralls pocket, and he fit a shiny brass key into the lock that secured the gate. "See this?" he said, holding the lock in a hand gloved in mahogany leather skin. "You can't find a padlock like this anymore. Anywhere. Fifty years of looking, and it's the only one of its kind. Solid cast bronze. Spring shackle. Rough finish. Seventy, seventy-five years ago it cost maybe, oh, maybe eight dollars. New. And eight dollars seventy-five years ago was a lot of dollars."

"How old?" the older boy (he'd been called Allan) asked.

"Seventy, seventy-five years."

"That's almost a hundred."

"Almost a hundred, that's right."

"Allan," the smaller boy said, "we ought to . . ."

The older boy whispered something into the ear of the younger and advanced through the open gate, to be followed, with pouting reluctance, by the younger boy, whose face was streaked with dust and apprehension.

"Come on inside," Horace said. He led the way, giddy almost to the point of dizziness at the prospect of entertaining guests. How long had it been since he'd invited or permitted another person into the house or the barn? Eighteen years ago . . . 1952. "The whole thing ought to come down." That was what the inspector had said when he'd finished examining the buildings. "It's all gonna collapse on you in six months." Horace had replied that if it did collapse, it wouldn't destroy anyone but him since no one else was ever inside. The inspector had closed his eyes and groaned when he'd checked the wiring. "I haven't seen these wires," he'd said. "Don't even whisper to anyone you showed them to me."

That had been eighteen years ago, and the barn and the house were both still standing. The inspector had been dead for nine years.

The boys leaned their bikes against the redwood tree. "Wow! How big around is this tree?"

One of those visitors from City Hall had asked the same question. After his friends had made several guesses and a few bets, one of the men had taken a tape measure from his pocket and had paced around the tree. "Thirty-four feet, nine inches," he'd said. Then they'd argued about how to find the thickness once they knew the circumference. There had been more discussion and more bets, and one of the men finally made the calculations. "Almost exactly twelve feet," he'd said, triumphant, since that had been the figure he had guessed. After he'd collected his winnings, he and the others had climbed into the station wagon with the Redwood County insignia on the doors. They'd driven off without a wave or a thank you.

"Well," Horace said, to the older boy, "that redwood is almost thirty-five feet around. Almost twelve feet through. Now you wait right where you are and I'll show you a trick."

He rushed into the house and found his mariner's sextant, the brass and copper device he'd dug out of Section F on the morning of the first anniversary of his arrival at the dump. He couldn't begin to guess how many hours had been spent smoothing and polishing the gears until they moved with the flick of a fingertip. His heart had skipped when he'd seen emerging from beneath the grease and corrosion the first faint trace of letters, then words. *The Good . . . The Good Ship . . . The Good Ship Celia!* And a second line beneath that line: *Good . . . Good Hope . . . Good Hope 11 Nov . . . Good Hope 11 November 1887.*

Eighteen eighty-seven! How old had he been in 1887? How long was it before 1887 that that Sunday . . . but no! It had been after 1887. And while he struggled with his calculations, Horace heard in the dim distance the whinny of a horse and the bark of a dog . . .

He turned and rushed outside.

"Either of you boys know what this is?"

They examined the instrument, turning it over and over in their hands, passing it back and forth.

"It's got these marks on it," the younger one said. "It measures things."

61

"That's right. But what does it measure?"

"It looks like one of those things sailors use," the older boy . . . Allan, that was his name . . . Allan said. "They measure where the stars are."

"Right. And do you know why they do that?"

"They can tell where they are by the stars," the young boy said.

"You young fellows are sharp as razors. You're right. It's called a sextant. Sailors use it to find their exact location. Degree of latitude, degree of longitude. That sort of thing. I used it to get the angle between the ground and the top of the redwood. Then I used some figures I got in a book inside the house and a formula some old Greek called Pythagoras figured out over two thousand years ago. And you know what?"

"What?" the young boy asked, fascinated now despite his fears.

"I figured out the height of the redwood almost to the foot, without leaving the ground or using a measuring tape."

The boys exchanged knowing glances, as if each were confirming the fact that they were being teased.

"I'm telling the truth," Horace said. "When you go back home and go to school tomorrow, you ask your teacher about something called trigonometry and a Greek named Pythagoras."

"We aren't going back home," the young one replied.

"Trigonometry," the older one said, after he had nudged his brother with an elbow, "that's mathematics. I'm good at mathematics."

"Right," Horace said. "It's mathematics. I learned it from a book."

"How tall is it?" the young boy asked, peering up into the tree.

"Almost exactly one hundred feet. Actually, last

62

time I measured it, three or four months ago maybe, it was ninety-seven feet."

"A hundred feet," Allan said. "Wow! I've never climbed that high, and I'm the champion climber in the whole school."

Horace laughed, stricken, then, with an urge to keep the boys with him. How could he lure them into staying the rest of the afternoon? If he weren't careful, they'd be rushing off as soon as they had their water. He pointed a finger at Allan. "You wanted some water. You're Allan. What's *your* name?"

"Samuel. Samuel Patrick Collins."

"Who was named Patrick in your family?"

"My grandfather. He had a big farm. In Ohio."

"Never been to Ohio. You ever been there?"

"No. Dad's gonna take us back. He . . . he keeps saying some day we'll go back. My grandfather's farm's still there and we still own it. My uncle takes care of it and . . ."

"Your friends don't call you Samuel. I bet they call you Sam. Anyway, that's what I'm gonna call you. My name's Horace. Horace Butright. I bet I'm the first Horace you ever met."

They thought about that, and then Allan said, "You are. You ever meet anyone named Allan?"

Horace pushed his San Francisco Giants ballcap back on his head, and after much chin-rubbing and head-scratching he said, "You know, you just might be the first and only Allan I ever did meet. But I've sure known a lot of Sams in my time." He watched Sam go to the redwood and try to put his arms around it. "My own personal redwood," Horace said. "The last one for miles. See those spikes sticking out of the trunk?"

Allan leaped, in an effort to catch the first spike, but no matter how high he leaped, the spike remained five or six feet above his fingertips.

"When I first got here fifty-nine years ago, I used to climb as high as I could go. Sometimes I'd set up there and watch the sun set. A couple times I've been up there to watch the sun rise. You can see the ocean from up there. I drove those spikes in with a sledge. They used to stick out about a foot and a half. Tree's gotten thicker. Only stick out about three, four inches now. Down at the base they're covered, grown over completely."

"I'd sure like to climb it," Allan said.

"Me, too," Sam said. Allan laughed and gave Sam a playful push. "I would," Sam said.

"Once," Horace said, "about fifteen years ago, I had a cat, Fatty Two . . . one I got now he's Fatty Three. . . . Lotta cats around here but old Fatty, he's special. Anyway, Fatty Two climbed up and wouldn't come down. I had to go up after her. That was my last climb."

"Doesn't it kill a tree when you hammer in spikes like that?"

"Not a redwood. Bark on this redwood is probably two feet thick before you get to the pulp. That's why redwoods live through forest fires so often. Thick bark saves them."

Sam was back at the tree, as if he couldn't quite believe it. He tried again to encircle the trunk with his arms.

"You look like you're trying to lift it out of the ground," Allan said. "Standing there like that, with your arms around it."

Sam, more than willing to play the role, grunted and pretended to lift.

"It's falling," Allan cried. He put his hands to his mouth. "Timber-r-r-r!"

Horace danced and skipped about, sharing the gag and the laughter. "OK," Horace said. "You asked how old it is. Well, I've been here for fifty-nine years, and it was almost six feet thick when I first came. I'd say it's over a hundred years old. Maybe over two hundred."

Allan let out a whispered "Wow!" and Sam whistled, or tried to. "Afterwards," Allan said, "after we get our drink, can I climb it? I really am the champion tree-climber. Ain't I, Sam?"

Sam nodded. "I'd like a drink, too," he said.

"Well," Horace said, "that's what a tree's for, for climbing. But come on inside first." They followed him through the door.

While Horace prepared a pitcher of Kool-Aid, the boys stood in the middle of the room, which meant . . . since the house consisted of one room . . . that they stood in the center of the house. Allan leaned sideways to steal a better view through the opposite door and into the barn.

"Wow," Allan said. "What is all this stuff? Where'd it come from? What are you gonna do with it all?" His and Sam's heads and eyes seemed to be the only parts of their bodies that were articulated.

"All these things yours?" Sam asked.

"All mine," Horace said, pouring the Kool-Aid into three clean jelly glasses.

"Look, Allan." Sam's shyness, or his fear . . . Horace was not sure which . . . was beginning to melt under the intensity of his curiosity.

"That," Horace said, returning the pitcher of water to the refrigerator, "is what women used when they wrung out clothes they washed. At the time they thought it was just about the fanciest invention since colored shoes."

"Wrung out?" Sam said, bending down to decipher the ornate black and gold print. "What do you mean?"

"Your mom probably has one of those fancy washing machines that does everything except fly her to Chicago. Right?"

65

Sam nodded and Allan said yes, it was fancy, but what did *this* thing do?

"Come with me," Horace said. "I'm gonna give you a history lesson."

Horace hurried into the barn. The boys, just as excited, ran to keep up with him. As he took them down aisles bordered with cartons and containers, odds and ends of machinery, clothing, books, cabinets stocked with watches and jewelry and dishes . . . the boys pointed and exclaimed. They stopped to examine something and then rushed to catch up, only to stop again . . . to point and exclaim and stop and rush again.

"Look . . . what's that? . . . Sam! Look! A lantern! An old police lantern! . . . Does this work. Horace? . . . Allan, there's a picture of these in my history book . . ."

At the end of one aisle two wooden tubs stood on fat little wooden legs. Horace tossed aside the cards fixed to each of the tubs with twine. Like every card on which he'd written, the words were for someone else, someone who some day might wonder what life had been like for a boy growing up in America before World War II, before World War I, before the sweeping second hand had converted . . . click! . . . the nineteenth century to the twentieth century. Since the cards were intended for someone else, the details had to be precise and organized.

"This one," he said, tapping one of the tubs, "is the Anthony Wayne Washer. This one over here's the Western Star. Both are made of white pine, both are painted and grained ash color. The staves . . . these boards . . . are corrugated. Remember that wringer you were looking at in the house? Here's where it goes, right here. Now" . . . and Horace took a deep breath . . . "remember what your mom does when she does a wash, and while you remember it, listen how women did the wash in the old days."

66

"Old days?" Allan asked. "How old?"

"Oh, seventy-five years ago. That old enough for you?"

"That's sure old enough," Sam said. "Grandma was seventy-two when she died."

"A spring chicken," Horace said. "Why, I bet she used one of these washers." Horace held up his hand, one finger extended. "First, evening before washday, all the clothes go into one big tub. Second, the tub's filled with rain water. Not water out of a tap, but rain water saved in a barrel. Third, clothes are soaked overnight. Fourth, next morning, the washboiler's filled three-fourths full with rain water. Fifth, you build a fire under the boiler and get the water boiling. Sixth, you cut one-half bar of hard soap into the water and one teaspoon washing fluid. Washing fluid's made by the woman, too. A pound of potash, one ounce salt of tartar, one ounce ammonia. The potash goes into a crock. Then a gallon of hot water's poured in, very slowly. When it's cool, the salt of tartar and ammonia go in. That's the washing fluid. Now, seventh, clothes are boiled ten to fifteen minutes, wrung out through the wringer in the house. Then, eighth, they go into a machine like this one, the Anthony Wayne or the Western Star. The machine works them ten, maybe fifteen minutes. Ninth, they're wrung out again and dropped in a basket. They're rinsed in clear water, tenth; wrung out again, eleventh; then, twelfth, they're hung outside on a clothesline to dry. One washing takes four or five hours. Now, you remember what your mom does when she does a wash?"

"She doesn't do the washing," Sam said. "Thelma does."

"Well, remember what Thelma does. She doesn't take four hours, she doesn't make her own soap. Who's Thelma? She your sister?"

"She's our . . ." Sam hesitated at the third word.

67

Allan supplied the word for him. "Thelma's our friend," he said.

"Thelma do all that work? Just to get your clothes washed?"

"I bet she used to. She used to live in Arkansas in the woods, and she didn't have a washing machine."

"She didn't have a toilet in the house," Sam said, obviously convinced that Horace would be shocked at the disclosure of such primitive conditions.

Horace obliged him. "Well, I'll be dadgummed. Where'd you say she lived? In the Amazon jungles?"

"No," Allan said. "In Arkansas."

When Horace shook his head in mock disbelief, Sam said, "It's true. I wish she could see this place. All the things you collected. Could we bring her sometime?"

Horace drew back. The request had been lurking, a crouching threat, at the back of his mind. Befriend these boys and they'll want to bring their friends. Then their friends' friends. It wouldn't stop. Before long the house and the barn would be overrun with strangers who'd be mauling and breaking and maybe even stealing every object that wasn't bolted down.

"Please?" Sam said. "I'd rather bring her than Mom or Dad or anyone."

No resisting a plea like that. Horace ran his fingers through Sam's still moist hair. "All right," he said. "Just Thelma. No one else. Come on back to the house."

At the wringer, back in the house, Horace took a towel from a drawer, soaked it with water, and ran it through the rollers. "You crank the wet clothes through with this crank. Like this." The towel moved through, appearing at the other side of the rollers pressed flat. "See? Got almost all the water out." He let the boys test the towel.

"How old did you say this is?" Allan asked, running the tips of his fingers across the rollers.

Horace pulled his hand away. "Watch it there. Many a woman's crushed her hands in those rollers." He smiled, to ease the concern that had flared on Allan's face when his hand had been grabbed. "Maybe seventy-five years old. Wringer's about the same. Of course, for its time, this one was real fancy. Had real steel ball bearings."

The wringer, perched on the table like a piece of sculpture, seemed to Horace to be preening itself under Allan's touch.

"Just finished painting it yesterday," Horace said. "Painted it exactly the way it was when it was new." The word *Cleveland,* in lean script, slanted across the mid-bar, just above the rollers. On the metal guide, which fed the wet clothes into the rollers, was the information, in square block print, THESE ALL WHITE RUBBER ROLLERS ARE VULCANIZED IMMOVABLY ON SHAFT.

Tied to one of the clamp screws protruding from the top bar, a three by five card described the unique features of the Cleveland wringer.

1. Turns with half the strength required for other wringers.

2. Cones and bearings made of steel, hardened and tempered.

3. Balls of hardened steel, same as are used in bicycles. Has wood frame, steel adjusting spring, two adjusting screws.

4. Price ... approx. $3.00

"Gee," Allan said. "It looks like it's brand new."

Horace giggled, his pink toothless gums flashing. "It ought to. Been working on it off and on for five years. Parts in there from twenty different wringers. But it's done. Way you see it's the way it looked and worked seventy-five years ago."

Sam had to sit on a chair and put his face close and admire the entire object, every screw and every stroke of paint. "Seventy-five years," Sam said. "What year was it seventy-five years ago?"

"Eighteen ninety-five," Allan said, gasping as he said it. "Wow! Thirty years after the Civil War ended."

"Right as rain. I was nine, maybe ten years old. Many's the time I saw my mother at a wringer exactly like that. Stand there by the hour, feeding in clothes. Hour after hour, dawn to dusk."

Horace turned away, to watch the gulls, a half mile away, climbing and floating over the garbage. "Hour after hour," Horace said, aware, as he spoke, that his mind had been drifting, dwelling again on the sounds of that summer Sunday and the vision of that empty porch with the two rockers and the call . . . almost a cry . . . *Horse . . . hey, you, Horse . . . Horace Butright . . .* carried on the breeze across the cornfield where he lay face down between the stalks, hiding. He shook his head, trying to disperse the memories that were fitting themselves into formation to attack. "I'm sorry," he said, knowing that Allan, who'd asked him a question, was still waiting for his answer. "I'm sorry. What did you say?"

"I said is everything here that old?"

Horace's eyes, and Allan's and Sam's, traveled over the objects that filled boxes lying on top of barrels and barrels stacked on top of boxes, that bulged out the sides of burlap bags and strained the staves of wooden crates, that spilled out of bins fixed to every wall of both the house and the barn. The house itself was so crowded that there was little room to sit or stand, but within the confusion everything seemed to have its place. Every loose item was labeled, and every container, bag or barrel or

70

crate or bin, was also labeled. Horace knew that at a moment's notice he could locate the jar or lid or hinge or gear or tool or handle or crank or book or strap he needed, retrieving it from the niche it might have been resting in for two weeks or twenty years.

"Some things, like me, are older. Me and that redwood tree are older than anything in the place."

Sam, sitting on an empty nail keg Horace had produced for him, said he bet he could guess how old Horace was.

"No need to guess," Horace said. "I'm eighty-five. Came here to this dump fifty-eight years ago. Was a man here then sort of took care of the place, name was Jacob Krebs. He died. I got his job. Been here ever since."

"Eighty-five," Allan said. "Wow! That's twice as old as Dad is. More than twice. He's not even forty-two yet."

"A mere baby," Horace said. His grin broke into a giggle, which exploded into a laugh. "I was forty-two, you know where I'd be? I'd be . . . well, I'd be right here, I guess." Of course he'd be right here. Where else was there to be? He listened. Was that Buster barking again? Was that the rustle of the corn again? Was that the call again? Listen . . .

"Horace, can we go in the barn?"

"Hmm? The barn? You want to go . . . sure, go ahead. Go in the barn. Look around. I got some sandwich meat. I'll make us some sandwiches and some more Kool-Aid. How about that? You boys hungry?"

"I'm starving," Sam said, drooping his shoulders and sticking out his tongue. "I bet I can eat five sandwiches."

"Come on, Sam. Let's explore."

Horace watched them dash down the aisle, flitting like two bees from one sweet temptation to another. Then he started making the sandwiches, singing a few

71

snatches of song as he worked. He stopped. What was that song he was singing? He couldn't recall the tune, but he had been singing. Had he ever sung before? It had to have been so long ago that it may as well have been never.

After making six sandwiches he cleared a space at the table and unearthed another nail keg and a stool.

The boys were in the corner of the barn where the wagons and surreys were stored. Allan had crawled into the seat of a surrey and was racing a team of imaginary horses down an imaginary road. Sam had located the cupboard of weapons, and he was aiming what looked like an Ithaca Ejector Hammerless. He swept the hide-outs on the far wall from left to right, shouting, "Ki-poo! Ki-poo! Ki-poo!"

Should he let them play another few minutes before he called them? Wasn't it almost more than a man could bear to hear such sounds, the voices of children at play?

Horace opened his mouth to call, but before a word could shape itself on his lips, he heard deep inside his head words he did not want to call, words he did not want to hear. *Horse . . . Horace, honey . . . it's time . . .*

He let the words drift through his mind, from ear to ear and eye to eye. "Time," he called. "It's time."

Chapter 5

Allan swished the Kool-Aid around in his mouth, wondering if he were the victim of some strange concoction . . . like those drugs he read about . . . that altered a person's vision. What else could explain the way Sam was acting?

Sam had not behaved with such animation since they'd been at summer camp. He asked Horace all sorts of questions and guessed at the answers before Horace could supply them, before Allan could parade his knowledge. Sometimes he answered the questions himself before he even finished asking them. And twice he reminded Allan that after they ate they'd climb the redwood tree.

When they'd first arrived at the dump, Sam had been so suspicious and frightened that he'd barely been willing to tell Horace his name. Now he was talking more rapidly, and louder, than Horace. Bouncing around on his nail keg, Sam gulped down his second sandwich and his fourth glass of Kool-Aid while Horace recited the

73

biography of a small fraction of the various items that had attracted the boys' interest. Though he spoke faster and faster and leaped from one thing to another, he failed to outdistance the questions that came mainly from Sam.

"This is an emery wheel dresser and it's . . ." ("What's an emery wheel? Where does emery come from?") . . . "I found this Geneva hand fluter last year in an old . . ." ("Why's it called Geneva, Horace?") . . . "The milk rooms were expensive. Cooley Creamers meant farmers could just do away with milk rooms . . ." ("Milk in bottles? Cream at the top of the milk? We don't get milk in bottles, Horace, we get it in wax cartons.") . . . ". . . a 400 candlepower, the strongest, best finished lamp a man could find. Perfect wick movement. See? Watch the wick . . ." ("What's a wick, Horace?")

Horace patiently interrupted his journeys from shelves to tables to counters to walls to answer every question. Often, before completing an answer to one question, he was off to another part of the room to return with something that provoked a new story and a whole new set of questions.

"This," Horace said, "is a sausage stuffer. *The Enterprise*. Name's right on it. *The Enterprise*. Farmers used it for all sorts of things besides making sausage, like pressing fruit or lard. Two-quart size had a rack movement. This one here is four quarts, got a screw movement. Cost about four dollars. Mostly butchers and housewives used the smaller ones. This goes up on the balcony in the barn, in Section M, Small Household. Got four barrels up in Section M filled with kitchen equipment like this. Cherry-stoners, raisin seeders, graters, slicers, meat choppers, jelly presses . . . and they all work, good as new. This sausage stuffer, the handle's broke. Gonna have to jump to find one the time I got left."

Nibbling the last crumbs of his sandwich and cast-

74

ing hopeful glances at the refrigerator, Sam went over to examine the sausage stuffer. Allan lifted a leather case from the enamel counter of a Hoosier cabinet. Setting the case on the table, he removed a small machine of oiled wood and polished brass. Horace answered his questions before he could ask them.

"Chisel grinder. Held chisels, plane irons, all kinds of blades like that. Ground them, sharpened them. You put the chisel right in there and you brought it up to the right bevel with the screw that's supposed to go right in there . . . in that hole. Been watching and waiting for just the right screw for five, six years. Now, you see, the blade's at the right level. You just bear down on the stone, grind . . . and whiz! . . . blade's sharp and smooth."

"I bet you could find a screw at Smith's hardware store in Orchid," Allan said. "They have a thousand different kinds of screws." So simple a solution, Allan was surprised that Horace hadn't thought of it.

Drawing back his hand and the chisel grinder as if he'd been slapped, Horace shook his head. "That's not the way." He seemed peeved. "The only screw goes in there is the screw meant to go there. I put in just any screw, a screw made in 1970, it ain't what it was seventy years ago. And that's what everything is here, the way it was seventy, seventy-five, eighty years ago, when I was as old as you are now."

Sam, back on his nail keg again, looked about for a napkin or a paper towel or a rag on which to wipe his hands. Horace reached over and took both hands between his own. He wiped them finger by finger on a leg of his crusted coveralls. Sam accepted his treatment, remaining sober all the while, until Horace caught his eyes and winked. And grinned. Sam leaped from his nail keg to investigate another surface, another fascinating object.

"I bet," Allan said, "I bet you'd rather be a boy then, when you were, than now. Being a boy now is like . . ."

"Like what?"

"It's like. I don't know. It's weird. It's like knowing that every night when you go to bed you're going to have a nightmare."

"Oh, Allan," Sam said. "You're always talking like that."

"In the old days," Allan said, "when there weren't things like big factories and big construction projects, was your dad home? He wasn't away all the time, was he? Did he talk to you? Go places with you? Did he . . . well, did he like you? Did you like him?"

Horace's eyelids closed very slowly over his blue eyes, and his attention returned to that small patch of coverall that had cleaned Sam's hands. His voice was so faint that Allan had to bend close to hear him.

"My father . . . he never yelled at me for anything. No one in the family ever raised their voices to one another . . . to anyone else. We loved each other. Sisters, brothers, mother, father, we loved each other. We sat and talked and sang songs together. A happy family, other people couldn't believe how happy we were together. After work, at the end of the day, my mother and father read us things. We had books. See up there on that shelf? And over there, that green set with gold lettering? Macaulay's *History of England*. Mother read to us from that. And *The Prairie* by James Fenimore Cooper. My mother read that. And Louisa Alcott. My father liked the Alger books . . . *Tom Temple's Career* and *Tom Thacher's Fortune* and *Tony the Tramp* and *The Train Boy*. Edgar Allan Poe's poetry, both my mother and father read Poe to us. And *Lorna Doone*. The best books. We talked about how to help each other, how we'd never leave each other, even when we grew up. We'd always be together."

Despite the movement of the old man's lips without an accompanied sound and the fix of the eyes on some distant target, Allan felt that in a moment the sound would return and Horace would continue describing his childhood. But the old man continued staring . . . not even his lips moving now . . . until the intense blueness of his eyes grew almost opaque.

"We ran away," Sam said, turning the chisel grinder over and over in his hands and running the tip of his finger across the emery surface.

Allan had hoped for some reaction . . . a lecture, criticism, praise . . . some indication that the act of running away from home deserved to be recognized as courage.

Horace's scuffed brown hands rose up slowly and then drifted down to the surface of the table. The movement of his arms must have triggered some mechanism in his brain because his eyes twitched and slowly dissolved the opacity and slowly fell into focus. They squinted at his hands, then shifted to the chisel grinder Sam was holding. "You ran away," he repeated, his voice, broken, unsure, dredged up from the depths of a dream.

"Yeah," Allan said, uneasy as the clear blue eyes shifted to his own to search there for some familiar landmark that might identify this place in which the old man was discovering the presence of strangers. Where had Horace wandered? To what mysterious shores had he traveled?

"You ran away from home?" Not so sleepy now, not so dreamy.

"Yeah," Allan said, wishing that Sam would forget the chisel grinder and say something, but Sam, preoccupied with the tool, was tilting it one way and then another, slipping it in and out of its holster. Sam responded to things, not to people. Like his father. A new piece of construction equipment was more exciting for his father than the marvelous talents a man brought to the controls to operate it.

His lips in a grim line over his toothless gums, Horace scowled at the implications of Allan's announcement. Menaced by the scowl and the quick, fleeting glare of the eyes, Allan searched for some new subject that might shift attention back to this room. "Can I climb the redwood tree now?" he asked.

Sam dropped the chisel grinder. "Can we? I bet we can see Orchid from the top. Can we, Horace?"

Horace nodded. "All right. But why did you . . .?"

"Sam, you don't want to climb."

Sam pushed back his nail keg and stood up. "I do." He ran to the door. "Come on, Horace."

Horace waved them on. "I'm coming, I'm coming."

Allan, with Sam at his heels, raced outside. The few gulls caught in the act of consuming yesterday's droppings leaped into the air and sailed off, to glide back to earth a few yards away. Across the dump, at Section E, thousands of other birds continued their loud and discordant dinner conversation.

Horace had said the lowest limbs of the redwood were more than twenty feet above the ground. To Allan, standing at the tree's base, they looked higher. The spikes Horace had pounded into the tree reached to those first limbs and beyond. "Horace, you have a ladder?"

"Sure do." Horace disappeared and soon reappeared with a long extension ladder. With the foot of the ladder on the ground, the top came to within a few inches of the first spike. "I'll tell you," Horace said,

78

"I'll tell you. You can bet I'd be right up there with you if these damn bones weren't so brittle."

Horace steadied the ladder while Allan climbed to the first spike. After eight more spikes he reached the first branch, which was about twice the thickness of his thigh. He sat on the branch and cupped his hands to his mouth and called down to Sam. "Come on, Sam. You said you'd climb."

Sam, standing at the third or fourth rung of the ladder, was not moving. He was staring up into the tree. Allan's brief sympathy gave way to anger. *Tough,* he thought. *You shouldn't have tried to impress Horace. Now you have to convince him you're not afraid.* Leaving Sam to his own problems, Allan continued his climb.

It was not too easy at first. The branches were sometimes only inches apart. The lateral twigs and branches locked together to form an almost impenetrable ceiling of green and brown. Allan closed his eyes, rammed his head up through the leaves and twigs and branches, and then pushed forward, his shoulders opening a passage through which he drew his body.

He stopped to rest. The branches were not so close together now. Looking down at the green jungle he'd been fighting through, he could no longer see the ground. He cupped his hands to his mouth. "You coming, Sam?"

The reply came from Horace. "You watch out now . . . don't you fall."

Sam was probably still on the same rung of the ladder. Well, he rarely even climbed that high.

Grabbing the limbs and pulling himself upward again, Allan felt that at any moment he would break through the branches and would find himself at the very tip of the tree. He wished he'd brought a knife. He'd have to think of a way to carve his initials in the highest branch.

"Come on, Sam," he called, "come on." He knew that Sam, far below, was regretting his hasty pretense at courage. Why had he ever tried?

Annoyance with Sam's phony courage evolved into anger, mild anger at first and then, feeding on itself, an intense anger. Why did he have to pretend he was something he wasn't? Charm, everyone praised him for his charm. But like his courage, his charm was phony, too. He could turn it on or off without thinking about it. A few minutes ago he'd wanted to impress Horace. And he'd been successful. Like most people, Horace had immediately been drawn to Sam. Well, maybe this was the time . . . today, here . . . maybe this was the time to put his brother in his fat, squidgy place.

As always, running parallel to Allan's anger was a sympathy that, at least until now, had always outlived the anger. He knew that when he returned to the ground, he would enjoy Sam's futile excuses for not having climbed the redwood, and then, charitable, protective, he would somehow manage to help lead Sam out of the trap he'd laid for himself.

What, Allan wondered, would Sam do if he, Allan, weren't there to lead? Why, for example, should it have been his responsibility to organize the escape from Orchid? Sam was just as unhappy at home as he was. Not so often, perhaps, but when he was, he didn't try to conceal it. He'd sit and sniffle, or he'd pout. And when Thelma, sensing his mood, would draw him close, to comfort him, he'd suggest, without saying it explicitly . . . no one said it explicitly any more . . . he'd suggest that things would be better if . . . if he and Allan lived . . . well, lived somewhere else. Thelma never took the bait.

When Allan stopped for his next rest, he thought less about Sam than he did about his own accomplishment. He'd climbed hundreds of trees, trees of all kinds and shapes and sizes, but he'd never climbed so high.

The foliage was thin enough now so that he could see across the dump to the freeway where he and Sam had been cursed by all those drivers. The wind that had been cool was now cold. He pressed his wet body against the trunk. Resting, he thought again about Sam. Content with his accomplishment, he could afford now to be more charitable. Poor old Sam. He wasn't responsible for the shape of his body (a daily target for jeers or laughter whenever he dared even a feeble attempt at softball or football or racing). If *he* were Sam, *he'd* not be so good-natured.

Was that what his mother meant when she said so often that he, Allan, ought to be more like Sam?

Ah, why did he have to think of her?

He grabbed a branch and continued climbing.

A single dark sea gull, suspended in the wind, flapped its wings twice and drifted close to investigate the intruder. It must have squawked, once, but the wind drowned out the sound. It veered sharply and fell away toward the ground, where . . . somewhere down there . . . was the house and the barn and Horace. And Sam.

Allan moved slower now, with less exhilaration. Were he to fall from this height, he would certainly die. The thought sent chills across his back. He'd stop climbing. But to stop now, so soon after that insight, would be an admission of cowardice. He continued on.

A second gull glided in, stared, opened and closed its beak. Its throat rippled. But all Allan heard was the rushing wind. He decided to start back down.

A deep breath first. One final view of the dump, the freeway, and, far away, the Pacific Ocean. Now he could begin his descent.

At that moment the green floor beneath him separated. A head appeared, shaking free of the twigs and green needle-like leaves. The head tilted, to expose a strangely familiar face. There were the full cheeks, the brown hair plastered to the high round forehead, and those wire braces on the teeth. But on the mouth that usually contained a mild, almost meek frown, there was now a grin of defiance, of accomplishment.

"Sam . . . you climbed up here?"

"I didn't . . . I didn't fly."

"I can't . . . I don't believe it."

"I do. I bet I sweated off ten pounds. You going higher?"

The last question, Allan decided, had to have been a trick of the snapping and growling wind. He couldn't possibly have heard what he thought he'd heard. "I'm coming down," Allan shouted.

And fat old Sam, still grinning, shouted back, "I'm coming up."

Even as he said it, he reached for the branch above his head and he hauled his body, awkwardly but successfully, up and onto the branch on which his pudgy hands had just been resting.

Looking up, Allan could see the top of the tree, this year's growth of feathery green, twenty or thirty feet above him. To climb any higher, he would have to rely on branches not much thicker than his own wrists. Were Sam to put his arms around the tree now, there would be no space between his hands, and his arms would overlap. Taking a deep breath, Allan climbed higher.

The tree swayed, and Allan, holding tightly with both arms to keep from being tossed free, squinted his eyes against the wind. The horizon, or what he could see of it when he could bear to look, tilted up and then down, down and then up, with what had just been *down* gliding *up* with sickening speed.

Now the limbs he stood on bent under his weight. He hugged the tree and shifted his feet closer to the vertical trunk. Sam, who'd had so little experience climbing trees, could not possibly know this trick, which shifted the stress away from that part of the branch least able to bear it. The wind brought tears to Allan's eyes, and in the tears Allan saw Sam stepping out too far from the trunk. He heard the branch crack. He saw Sam's body hurtling down through green space. Falling, tumbling, striking, and bouching from branch to branch. Landing, finally, *thud!* . . . on the ground. *Dead!*

"We can't go any higher," Allan shouted.

"Sure we can." Sam's voice came from directly beneath Allan's feet. Allan closed his eyes until the tears cleared, and then he saw Sam's head moving up . . . up toward his feet.

"Sam . . . you better not climb . . . you've never been this high . . . you don't know how to . . ."

"I'm going higher."

And Allan could only watch as Sam's body, on the opposite side of the trunk, inched upward, until the fat wet face was hovering there directly opposite his own.

"Sam! The tree won't hold us both. If you go any higher . . ."

The combined weights of their bodies tipped the trunk so far that once, opening his eyes, Allan looked up into the clouds. He closed his eyes, and his breath froze in his throat. He dared not open his eyes, he dared not move an inch. Sam was moving past him, past and above him. Allan opened his eyes. Finger by finger, hand by hand, Sam moved up the shaggy red trunk toward the new green growth waving in the sunlight.

The faded, torn jeans slipped by, scratching and sliding on the bark. There, an inch from his eyes, were Sam's knees, bruised and bloody, framed in the holes in the jeans. The knees moved past. And there were Sam's sneakers, laces so sloppily tied they were almost loose, gouging the trunk for a foothold.

Furious, wanting to scream, wanting to plead, Allan could only groan and clutch the tree more tightly.

"I'm going down." Allan was not sure whether he'd spoken or thought the words, but he began his descent.

After what seemed like hours but could only have been minutes, he reached a branch thick enough to hold them both. He stopped and sat close to the trunk. The chunks of bark torn free by Sam's feet struck his head and his neck. He didn't care. He had to rest. Why was he trembling? Had he been that terrified? No, it wasn't just terror that had shocked and frightened him. Sam. Sam had shocked him. And frightened him. Why had he done it? Why?

He lay his head back. Sam's feet appeared, then his legs, then his upper body. His T-shirt, black and torn, was smeared with blood from countless scratches and bruises, but his face was almost split open with a wild grin. For one brief moment (his arm actually jerked into action before he caught and stopped it) Allan wanted to reach out and wipe the grin from Sam's face with his hands. Instead, he looked down. "I wonder if Horace is still waiting."

Sam sat on the branch above him. He was gasping. "I sure wish . . . I had . . . some of the things he has."

"I wonder if he'd let us stay here," Allan said. He knew Sam must be wondering why he'd made no comment about his climb, but he didn't dare talk about it. Not yet.

"You mean just for tonight?"

"No, I meant for maybe a couple weeks."

"He must get lonely," Sam said, "way out here by himself."

Why wasn't Sam talking about his climb? Was he trying to impress Allan with his humility?

Allan walked out toward the end of the branch, holding discreetly to the branch above. In a demonstration

84

for Sam's benefit, which did not go unnoticed, he walked far beyond the safe point. "Mom and Dad wouldn't let us," Allan said. "But that doesn't matter anymore." How would Sam respond to that?

"Yeah. We can go where we want to and stay as long as we want. Just like you said, Al."

"Right. We can do anything we want to now."

"Al."

"Yeah?"

"I'm glad we ran away. I am now. For a while, though . . ."

Allan waited, unwilling to help. If Sam had found the courage to drag his fat body up that tree, he could damn well find the courage to say what he felt. *I*, Allan insisted to himself, *am not going to put the words in his mouth*. He has to find his own words now. He has to make his own decisions now.

"He never does what he promises."

"Who doesn't?" Allan asked, taking one more step along the limb that bent even farther beneath him. Yes, he saw, Sam was watching.

"Dad."

"What do you mean?"

"Well, like the *Kennedy*. He's been saying he'll help me for almost a month now. And remember last April? When he promised we'd go down the Colorado River in the summer? On a raft? Remember?"

"So we went to camp instead. You liked camp." Still holding to the overhead branch, he eased his feet a few inches forward. He listened for the telltale sounds of strain and prayed his judgment would be correct. If he did not step back in time, Sam *would* have to settle his problems by himself. Along with the fear that brought the sweat popping out of his armpits came a sensation that he alone was determining now not just his own fate but that of Sam as well. Fear and pride, fear and strength, fear and courage. It took courage to make decisions not just about your fate but also about someone else's.

"OK, I liked camp. So what? You know what I mean."

"How should I know what you mean?"

Dig it out, damn you. Say it. If Sam was to determine his own life, let him start now.

"And the rabbits. He promised them to me."

"They were dirty."

"That's what he said. After he promised them to me. And Mom, too. For my birthday. She promised, too. Why'd they have to *promise?*"

"If the rabbits chewed up the flowers or messed up the lawn, there wouldn't be all those pictures in the newspapers."

"Who cares about that?"

"Mom cares."

"Yeah. She sure does. That house. I wished we lived in a shack. I wish Dad just had a job like . . . like Horace has. One thing, we won't have to hear about the house all the time, and we won't have to go on those stupid picnics every Sunday." Allan heard the break in Sam's voice. "I wish they'd . . . I wish they'd . . ."

Careful. He'd been led to the point where he almost had to speak out. Would he?

Sam gulped and rubbed his eyes. "You better not go out any farther, Al. Please don't."

Allan eased backward, turned, and scurried along the branch. "Let's go," he called, swinging down through the branches, dropping easily and rapidly, knowing that Sam could not possibly match his agility. He stopped when he was in sight of the last branch between him and the ground and waited there until Sam, grunting and groaning, appeared.

Horace was lying on the ground, the ladder beside him. "Horace! Hey, Horace!"

86

Horace sat up, looked around, and then, when Allan called his name again, he looked up into the tree.

Sam dropped onto the branch beside Allan. "Hi, Horace. We got clear to the top almost."

Allan waited for Horace to set the ladder in position, thinking all the while: Sam had said *we*. He'd said, "*We* got clear to the top."

Chapter 6

The white T-shirts flashed like anxious birds high in the green-black mass of the redwood, and voices, shrill and high-pitched, sharp as bird calls, drifted down through the air. Horace closed his eyes again. How long had he been lying here? He'd been sleeping. How long ago had the boys started their climb? He had no idea. Had he always had such difficulty distinguishing minutes from hours, one day from another, one week from the next?

The voices grew louder and the flashes of white T-shirt clearer and closer. What would he do if one of the boys *fell,* was seriously hurt and had to be taken to the hospital? How would he get him there? If he had a phone, he'd be able to call for help. But he had no phone.

The Board of Supervisors should have brought the phone to the house last year, when they'd promised it. There ought to be a phone at the County Dump, so people could call if they had any questions. One of the supervisors, during that visit, had said that all arguments about whether there should or should not be a phone were academic anyway. Before Horace could ask for an explanation, one of the men had reminded the group they were late and had better leave.

Horace stood and leaned close against the redwood. Surely, by now, the boys had reached the top of the tree or were as close to the top as they could climb. He knew how they felt, being a part of a tree that had probably witnessed massacres and stampedes and fires and floods and droughts, and a hundred other natural and man-made disasters. That day he'd climbed to rescue Fatty Two, he'd lingered on the branch from which he'd plucked the cat. With Fatty secure in the knapsack on his back, he'd been about to start down when he'd thought: *This is the last time I'll ever climb this tree.* He'd stood on the limb, looking out toward the ocean, trying hard to convince himself that it didn't matter, that growing old and failing to achieve a dream weren't important. Then, with one last long look at the ocean and one last long look at the desert of mud and garbage and debris, he'd sighed and said, "Well, Fatty, we have to go."

Horace picked at the coarse red-brown bark, lifting strings of moss from the deep dark troughs, his hands so rough and scarred that they might have been hewn from the bark itself.

He patted the tree. How'd we do it, friend? You and me, how'd we make it?

In the years he had worked and walked and slept under this redwood tree, there had developed that sort of relationship in which old friends overlook each other's vices while taking each other's virtues for granted; neither one, in the process, noticing the other's growing old. What, Horace wondered, had been the strange complex of events that had converted those hills to these valleys, that had permitted this single redwood to survive in a stretch of land where all others had perished?

Horace kneeled in the spongy topsoil formed of a century's accumulation of tree droppings. He fitted his hands over a fragment of the gnarled base. His body fell back to a sitting position, his right side against the tree. If only he'd had the youth and the strength to have accompanied the boys, to have stood once more at the top of the tree. . . . If only. If . . . if . . .

A piece of bark, broken free by the foot or hand of one of the boys, struck his face. He heard their laughter, their calls to each other. And he heard his own name. "Horace! Hey, Horace . . ."

Horse . . . hey, you, Horse . . .

No longer a desert of garbage and debris in front of him, only a vast and endless stretch of green, of green corn . . . green corn rustling.

Horse, honey, it's time . . .

He struggled against the lure of that voice, knowing that each time he'd yielded in the past, the remorse that had followed had proven more intense.

And there it was, the green again, the green field of corn. Again. *Stalks and leaves clicking together like twenty dragons gnashing a thousand teeth. And there was Buster, barking, no longer down by the pond but closer now. And Lady whinnying in the sweet alfalfa in the meadow. And Mrs. Kilpatrick calling from the porch: "Horse, honey, they're here." He rolled over onto his belly, praying that he not be found. But Buster pounced at him, licking his face, and Mr. Kilpatrick pushed the stalks aside. "There you are. Come on, boy. You got to go." He tried not to cry. "Don't cry, Horse." Lifted, he was carried through the corn, the broad, sharp-edged leaves reaching for a farewell touch of his body. The road wagon waited near the gate. The bay mare's head drooped in her traces. A small carton of his clothes had already been deposited behind the seat in which the*

90

man and woman sat. "Horse, this is Mr. and Mrs.
Pendergast." Mrs. Kilpatrick, weeping . . .

"Horace. Hey, Horace, we need the ladder."

Grinning like Humpty Dumpty, a boy on the bottom
limb of the redwood was dropping pieces of bark on
Horace's chest. Another boy, not so round and not grinning, sat beside Humpty Dumpty.

"Horace, we need the ladder to get down."

Allan, that was it. Allan and . . . what was the
younger one's name?

He put the ladder against the tree. Allan came down
first, and the other . . . Sam, that was it! . . . Sam, close
behind, slipped and tumbled the last few rungs, knock-
ing Allan to the ground. The boys giggled and wrestled
until Horace asked them if they'd been calling him very
long.

"Yeah," Allan said, lifting himself by pushing
down on Sam's paunch. "About five minutes. Boy, you
sure do sleep."

When Horace carried the ladder around the side
of the house, the boys followed him, arguing about how
high they'd been when they'd quit climbing. As he
slung the ladder onto its brackets, Horace wondered if
he hadn't . . . without intending it . . . chosen favorites.
Allan, for him, was a touch too sober, too mature. Without too much effort he could become a bully. Sam could
not be pretentious if he tried; he was naturally open,
naturally spontaneous and silly, without malice.

The two of them were arguing now about the thickness of the tree trunk when they'd stopped climbing.
"It was this thick," Allan said, running ahead of Horace
and turning to hold his hands about a foot apart.

"It was this thick," Sam said, his own hands less
than six inches apart.

Allan ridiculed that, saying that if it had been so

91

small, it would have broken. Sam said well, OK, it might not have been as thin as he said, but it wasn't as thick as Allan was saying either.

"It looks to me," Horace said, "like you climbed to different heights."

The boys grew strangely subdued. Sam lowered his eyes and kicked at a stone. He shuffled toward the front door while keeping an eye on his bike, as if without too much provocation he might just leap on the seat and ride off. Allan stuck out his chin and pinched his lips together and seemed to find a certain crippled gull a subject of endless fascination.

"Sam climbed higher," Allan said. He ran past Sam and entered the house. Sam seemed reluctant to enter. Horace held the door open. Sam kicked at the dirt.

"Come on in," Horace said. "You must be hungrier than ever. How about some peanut butter and . . ."

The bait worked. Sam turned from the bike and came inside. He sat across from Allan, but they both kept their eyes down. Their faces were still wet with perspiration, and their clothes were damp. "How about some Kool-Aid," Horace said, "while I make us some peanut butter sandwiches. You have to drink lots of fluids. Good for your system. Flushes out the poisons." He filled their glasses from the dented aluminum pitcher and then made the sandwiches. Each of the boys, while they waited, downed two glasses of the cherry-flavored drink. In the quiet interlude Horace pretended not to notice Sam nudging his brother.

Allan cleared his throat, set his glass down, and said, "Horace."

"Yeah?"

"Can we live here with you? We can work and help you."

Sam, who'd been nodding vigorously as Allan talked, said, "I'm good at fixing things. Ask Allan."

92

Horace sipped his drink. He'd not believed them when they'd said something about running away from home. In fact, he was not sure whether he'd heard it or imagined it. Had he been *hoping* they'd ask to stay? Since they'd been here, he'd sensed more strongly than ever the acute loneliness of his life. Ah, if they were his own sons! Even Allan, whose quiet, almost sullen manner seemed balanced by a devotion to his brother . . . even Allan appealed so strongly to Horace that he wanted to embrace the boy. "Did you boys say you ran away?" Horace asked.

Allan nodded and Sam said, "Sure we did."

"Why?"

"Because," Sam said. He appealed to Allan, as if Allan could express their reasons more clearly. ·

"We were bored," Allan said.

"Bored? You ran away because you were *bored?*"

Sam shifted, uncomfortable. Allan shrugged. "You wouldn't understand. No one would. It wasn't just because we were bored, it was . . . well, I can't explain."

"Can't explain? What kind of answer is that? Any boy who runs away from home has to have a better reason than he was *bored.*"

"Didn't you ever run away from home?" Allan asked.

"No. Home ran away from me."

"Home ran away from you? What's that mean?"

The words had popped out. But that was what had happened!

Bored. Can you imagine being bored with a mother and father there, right in the house, every night when you go to bed and there in the house every morning when you wake up? Oh, if they only knew, if he could only tell them. *They* had a home! They had a mother! They had a father! They had each other.

. . . *Mrs. Kilpatrick, weeping, her apron up over her*

93

face, turned to rush back into the kitchen, but stopped. She turned to hug him, to kiss him again. With her apron once more up over her face, she ran into the house. She did not return this time. "Let's go, son," Mr. Pendergast said. Mr. Kilpatrick lifted him onto the wagon. The mare raised her head at the snap of the switch, and the wagon moved down the road. He did not look back at the fifth house (not home but house) in which he had lived since he was four years old. (Or was it three? Or was it five? He'd never known and he'd never know.) The last sound he heard from that last house was Lady whinnying (crying?) from the meadow where, yesterday, before he'd been told he'd again be leaving to live with yet another family, he'd kissed her velvet nose and fed her apples. Softly, tenderly, she had nuzzled the skin of his palm, taking care not to hurt him or frighten him.

"Horace, you just spread peanut butter all over your hand." Both boys were laughing.

Horace looked down. Yes, he'd missed the slice of bread, he'd spread the peanut butter over the back of his hand.

"Bored?" Horace said. "Don't you have friends?"

"Sure we have friends. It's the same with them. We all talk about running away some day, but Sam and me, we did it."

"What about your folks?"

Allan dismissed the question with a wave of his hands. "They don't care. They say they do, they think they do, but they don't care."

Horace shook his head, freeing himself from the distracting thoughts of that summer Sunday. "They feed and clothe you, don't they? From what you say, you got a fancy home. Who bought you those bikes? And that fishing gear? Did *you* have to pay for those things?"

"We have the fanciest home in Orchid," Sam said.

94

"That's what Mom always says. There were pictures in all the newspapers and magazines. You see them?"

"I don't read magazines or newspapers. Long time ago I did. I got whole shelves full of magazines and catalogues and newspapers from when I was a boy the same age as you."

How would the boys react if they saw those magazines? Would they laugh? Well, it was all right if they did. Sometimes, when he leafed through a catalogue and saw the world of 1900 . . . of 1890 . . . of 1880 . . . a world so simple, so safe, he wondered why the motor was invented. More than once, stopping at an ad for a cobbler's unit or a harness-mending outfit or a Brownie suit for children . . .

No. 4612 Blue Denim Brownie Suit for 28¢. Made of a good quality blue denim. Just the thing for a boy's everyday go-as-you-please suit.

No. 4614 Gray Striped Brownie Suit for 35¢. Let your boy play in the healthy outdoor air this summer dressed in a Brownie suit. They are all the style this season.

. . . more than once his eyes had filled not with tears of pain but with tears of pleasure.

"Do you love them?" he asked.

"Mom and Dad?" Sam said. "Of course I love them."

Allan's "No" had preceded Sam's "Of course" by a fraction of a second. "I don't even like them," Allan said. He turned on Sam, his expression severe, almost contemptuous. "Neither do you, Sam. You won't say so, but you don't."

Sam, uneasy, tried to avoid a decision. "Aw, you always exaggerate, Allan."

"OK, if you had your choice, would you rather live with Mom and Dad or with Thelma?"

"Who is this Thelma woman?" Horace said.

"She works at our house," Allan said. "This summer, when we came home from camp, Mom and Dad weren't there, but she was. Dad's a contractor. Mom and Dad were at a contractors' convention in Hawaii. They didn't see us all summer, and when we came home, they weren't even there. And you were glad, Sam. We celebrated. We both jumped in the pool. Thelma was there and . . ."

"You're not fair," Sam said. "You oughtn't to talk like that about Mom and Dad." He rubbed his eyes, and his lower lip began to quiver.

"Don't go and cry now."

"I'm not gonna cry."

"Go ahead," Horace said. "You want to cry, you go ahead and cry."

"I don't want to."

At that moment Horace was so upset that he almost asked them to leave. They'd succeeded in catching him up in the troubles outside the fence, beyond Anders Corners, and he didn't have time for such distractions. He'd made a decision that, for as long as he lived, he would concentrate on this house, on this barn, on these artifacts of his childhood. *His* childhood? How could he pretend that these . . .

There! He was already questioning . . .

Careful. He had to be careful or he would divert to Sam and Allan the hostility he had reserved all these years for the patrons of the dump, for the busybodies at Anders Corners, for the entire human race.

That did it.

The boys had to go home. They had to go right now. But before they went, they had to know . . . he had to somehow enlighten them about that special terror that waits for the man . . . or the boy . . . who cuts himself off from those he loves, from those who love him.

96

"I'm gonna do something," Horace said. "You won't like it, but I'm gonna do it anyway. I'm gonna drive you to Anders Corners. If that maverick old Ford will take us that far. You're gonna call your folks and you're gonna tell them where you are. They're worried. I know they are. They're reminding each other how wrong they've been. Promising each other if you're only found safe, they'll do better. You gotta go back. You'll tell them where you are, and they'll come running to get you." And then, his voice hoarse, on the verge of breaking, Horace said, "You can't make me believe your own mother, your own father, don't love you. You can't make me believe it. You can't."

The boys sat through his lecture without responding, without the slightest indication that they were disappointed or angry or even that they had heard. Horace blew his nose into a big blue handkerchief. He sat on a stool. "Look at me," he ordered. "You probably think I'm betraying you. I'm not, I'm doing you a favor. A big favor. You won't know, for a long time, for many years, how big a favor. I'm telling you the truth. They love you, they *have* to love you. They can't *not* love you. Even if they don't want to, they *have* to. That's the way mothers and fathers are. They're human, they just *have* to be that way. If they weren't . . . well, if they weren't that way, they wouldn't be human. Would they?"

Sam began to sniff. Allan sat with his forehead in his hands. Was he hiding his tears? Why should he be ashamed to let his tears be seen? Horace reached over to tug at his wrists, but Allan outmaneuvered him and shifted his body beyond reach. "Boys, I'm sorry. I know how you feel. But I'm taking you back if it's the last thing I ever do. No two ways about it. It's getting late. Another two hours it'll be dark. We'll pack your bikes in the truck bed."

Sam was muttering, "Come on, Allan, come on."

Allan, ignoring him, stared bleakly at the floor.

"Tell you what," Horace said. "As a sort of reminder of today, the fun we had, why don't you pick something? Both of you. Anything. In the house or the barn. Maybe, when you're grown up, when you have your own kids, you can show them whatever you pick out here. You can tell them stories about that crazy old coot you met one Sunday when you were boys. You can tell them how you climbed to the top of one of the very last redwood trees in Redwood County . . . maybe it will be the last one by then . . . and you can tell them about the old geezer who gave you . . . well, he gave you something to remember him. How about it?"

Sam said, "I want to go back, Allan."

Allan shrugged and stood up.

"Will you pick out something?" Horace asked.

"Anything?" Sam said. "Really anything?"

"Anything. Of course we have to be able to get it in the truck." Horace got up, hoping his movement would stir Allan into motion.

"Come on," Sam said, leading Horace into the barn. They went down one aisle after another, with Sam's appraising eye missing nothing.

Allan, Horace noticed, remained in the house, by the door. Maybe, after Sam made his selection, Allan would weaken.

"Can I have that?"

Horace smiled. "You got a good eye." He lifted the object and showed Sam one of the three cards tied to it. "Can you read what it says?"

"Stereo . . . gra . . . graph . . . grapho . . . scope."

"Right," Horace said. To save Sam from embarrassment, he read each of the three cards aloud. Sam, his eyes glued to the gift he'd selected, was attentive to every word. "Stereographoscope. Combination stereoscope

98

and graphoscope. Magnifies single or stereoscopic pictures. For graphoscope, lens are reversed. Made of oiled and polished cherrywood. Folding box, ebonized finish. Fine quality four-inch lenses for graphoscope views. Two stereoscope lenses. Approximate price: four dollars and twenty-five cents." Horace held out the box. "Samuel Patrick Collins, you made a fine choice. This happens to be one of my personal favorites. Many a night my mother and father and my brothers and sisters . . . we sat . . . we . . ."

He interrupted himself to listen. No doubt about it. The bark was Buster's. And that call from the porch: *Horse, honey, they're here . . .*

"Can I have some of these?" Sam said, opening a second leather box that contained four rows of slides. He fitted one of the slides into the holder and aimed the viewer at the light. "Wow! Look, Horace!"

Horace managed to lift the viewer to his eyes.

"It's Yellowstone National Park," Sam said.

"Yellowstone National Park," Horace said.

"It says so on the box."

"Take the whole box," Horace said. "It fits right inside the big box."

"The whole box? Wow!" And Sam read aloud the label on the leather lid. "Ster . . . stereo . . . scop . . . ic views. Highest grade made. Size four ex seven inches . . ."

"That means four *by* seven inches."

"Four by seven inches. On heavy mounts. All taken from original negatives. Sporting series, hunting, fishing, canoeing, camping scenes, and life in the woods. Yellowstone National Park with hot springs, geysers, falls, and so forth. Alaska, the Land of the Midnight Sun, the glaciers, mountains, Indian life, totem poles. Florida, tropical scenes. Niagara Falls in summer and winter. Dells of Wisconsin. World's Fair with realistic views of the fairground, buildings, the Midway." Sam took a deep breath. "Thanks, Horace."

"You're welcome, Sam." Horace knew that if he stayed here one more moment, with Sam peering up at him like that, he would say they could stay at the dump for as long as they wished. "We better go," he said, hurrying out of the barn.

Allan was outside. He'd lifted both bikes into the bed of the pickup, and he was leaning against the tailgate, watching three gulls fight for a gray crust of bread.

Sam rushed to show Allan his gift, but Allan turned aside, to climb into the front seat. Sam, chattering away, carrying the black box close to his chest, climbed in beside him.

Horace walked to the gate. If he opened it now, he wouldn't have to get out of the truck twice, to open *and* close the gate. What would he do, he wondered, when he got to Anders Corners? He didn't like the idea of just dumping the boys at a curb, but what choice did he have? If he waited too long, it would be dark. And he couldn't drive without headlights. "Wearing out," he said with a sigh, as he settled himself behind the steering wheel. "Wearing out. No more spare parts."

The clock in the kitchen had shown the time to be ten minutes past four o'clock. If the truck gave no trouble, he could have the boys in Anders Corners by five. It would be too dark to drive by six-thirty, which meant he'd have to leave Anders Corners immediately. Well, no use wasting time.

He adjusted the choke and the gas feed and he stepped on the starter. The motor coughed, gasped and caught, promised to stay alive and then died. The second time it kept its promise, shaking and rattling the entire truck as it idled. "She doesn't move in any gear but first,"

100

Horace said. "So we won't get arrested for speeding."

The truck moved out of its rut and then, once out, it coughed again and almost stalled. Horace, slapping the accelerator, bouncing and grunting, convinced it to move, slowly, toward the gate. It coughed and shuddered, as if the movement from the space in which it had rested for so many weeks had required its total store of energy.

Once through the gate, Horace knew that he dare not chance letting the motor idle and setting the hand brake. "Sam, you better get out and lock the gate. Shake it and make sure you can't spring the lock after it's closed.

Sam leaped out, anxious to prove his competence. Horace leaned forward, trying to catch Allan's eye, but Allan seemed unaware of his presence. "Gonna be a bumpy ride," Horace said. "This ain't no Pierce Arrow." Allan did not respond. "You ever see a Pierce Arrow?"

"No."

"Well, neither did I. It's supposed to be the fanciest car ever." Grateful for Sam's return and his assurance that the gate was securely locked, Horace eased out the clutch. The truck bucked twice and then crawled forward.

Neither Sam nor Allan made a sound as the truck fought its way up the dirt road and along the asphalt highway.

"Allan," Horace said, "are you mad because I'm taking you back?"

"I'm glad we're going back," Sam said. "I bet you are, too, Allan."

"You're stupid!" Allan shouted.

"I can stop," Horace said. "I can drop you off. You want to go on alone?"

"OK, let me out."

"No," Sam cried. "No, Allan. Please don't."

All of a sudden, in one moment, Allan crumbled,

101

falling over, his face pressed into Horace's coveralls. "I want to stay with you. If . . . if I can't stay with you . . . OK, I'll go . . . go home."

Horace gripped the steering wheel with one hand and patted Allan's shoulder with the other. "You wouldn't like staying with me. I might like it, for a while, then pretty soon I might not like it. I'm . . . I'm sort of strange. And the law. Your mom and dad wouldn't let you stay. The law . . . well, it just wouldn't work. Trust me, Allan. Just trust old Horace. I know your folks will understand if you tell them what's wrong. Try it. For me. Will you?"

Allan sat up. He rubbed his eyes and nodded.

"I know how you feel," Horace said.

"*I know how you feel.*" *Mrs. Pendergast said, reaching back to touch his arm.* "*Go ahead, son, you go ahead and have a good cry. I know how you feel.*"

"*Don't make a crybaby out of him,*" *Mr. Pendergast said.* "*It's rough enough. If he's a crybaby, it'll be rougher. They promised he was grown and a good worker.*"

"*Grown?*" *Mrs. Pendergast said.* "*He's a boy. A child. My father used to say: 'Poverty comes in through the window, love goes out through the door.'*"

"*You start gushin' all over him,*" *Mr. Pendergast said, "you'll ruin him.*"

"Ruin who?" Allan said.

"What?"

"Ruin who? You said something that sounded like *you'll ruin him.*"

"I did?"

"Yeah. Ruin who?"

"No one," Horace said. "Now, Sam, that stereoscope, that's for both of you. That understood?"

"Understood," Sam said. "Allan? That understood?"

102

"Understood," Allan said. "Horace, next Saturday . . . hey, Horace."

He waited until they were asleep, and then he dressed in the dark. The two collies followed him to the gate, which he opened with care, so the collies didn't escape. He ran until he was exhausted. He fell and lay where he'd fallen. When he opened his eyes, the sun was sliding up over the horizon. From somewhere beyond the cornfield came the steady rumble of a freight train and the engine's whistle. He rose and stumbled toward the sound. No more aunts, he vowed. No more uncles. No more. Somewhere on the other side of the darkness he would find them, those parents, who, unable to afford him, afford to love him, had run away from him before he had learned to recognize their faces or their voices. They were there, somewhere on the other side of the darkness, waiting for him, ready to explain, to beg forgiveness. He would rush to forgive them, and they would embrace each other, and he would gorge himself on their love.

"Hey, Horace, you know that for about a mile now you've been in the wrong lane?"

He jerked the wheel, and they sped toward the ditch at the right side of the road, but at the last moment he swung back, into the wrong lane, then to the right side. Finally he settled in the correct lane. "Understood?"

Both boys replied, in unison, "Understood."

Chapter 7

Pressed in on one side by a tense and sober Allan and on the other by the hard, cold metal door, Sam played games with the oncoming cars. He stared back at the faces that stared at him through their windshields or side windows. He grinned back at the grinning faces or wrinkled up his nose and stuck out his tongue at the taunting faces. Horace, his sight fixed on the white line, drove as if the battered old Ford were the only vehicle on the road, devoting equal respect to right lane, left lane, white center line.

They picked up speed on the downslopes. "Free wheeling," Horace said, slipping the gearshift into neutral. "Saves gas."

The speedometer needle flipped between zero and twenty, stopping at one of the two but never in between. "I'd guess we must be hitting twenty-five, at least, going downhill," Horace said. When no one commented, he added, "On the level it must be around ten. Maybe even twelve."

104

Climbing a steep hill, they traveled along at a noisy, gear-grinding pace that would never show, Horace promised, on any speedometer, even if it worked. "You know," Horace said, "I got this truck maybe fifteen years ago. It's older than fifteen, but I got it fifteen years ago."

"Where?" Sam asked.

"Well, used to be I had cars and trucks at the dump. But they took up too much space. About fifteen years ago the county supervisors said I wasn't running a junkyard, I was running a dump. Now the cars and trucks go down south, a place where they're crushed into lumps of metal about the size of a bale of hay. Used to be . . . twenty, twenty-five years ago . . . used to be lots of trucks around like this one. Started taking them apart in my spare time just to learn what made them go. Got to be a pretty fair mechanic. Put the good pieces from all the trucks into one . . . this one. Started driving around the dump and then into town. Never did get a license."

Allan's head was back on the seat, his eyes half closed.

Maybe, Sam thought, *it isn't just our going home. Maybe he's still thinking about today, about how I climbed higher than he did. Maybe it's because he cried just now. I've never seen him cry.*

Like all their friends, Sam admired Allan not just because he was older or bigger but because he was more courageous than anyone else. He took chances none of the others dared take, whether it was climbing trees, swinging from one tree to another, diving off the high board at Camp Gualala, or fighting anyone who felt compelled to challenge his leadership. That time he'd broken his arm at the baseball game he'd played the last two innings and walked home without complaining. Last year, when he'd been called into Mr. St. Clair's office

105

and threatened with dismissal if he didn't tell who'd released the air from the tires of all the cars in the teachers' parking lot, he'd refused to say a word. And he'd not been dismissed.

He was just as brave . . . if brave was the word . . . at home. Allan often said the things Sam was reluctant to say, though, quite often, he wanted very much to say them. Like talking back to his father. Or using the words he knew his mother did not like to hear. Though he was impressed by Allan's bravado, Sam was also very often distressed. He knew Allan enjoyed the grunt of surprise or the sudden expression of shock that would appear, unwittingly, on his mother's or father's face when he said or did something that Sam said or did in the privacy of his room, behind the closed door. Allan never seemed aware of Sam's envy. Or maybe, Sam thought, he knew but just didn't care.

Today, for once, Allan had had a large dose of Sam's frequent medicine: envy. For once it had been Allan who'd followed and Sam who'd led.

Sitting in the seat of the groaning, chugging, barely moving truck, it was Sam's turn to be moved by compassion for his brother. He'd known envy and hostility and often, too often, he'd known admiration for Allan. But he'd never known compassion.

"Al?"

"Yeah?"

"If you don't want to go home, I won't go."

Horace leaned over the steering wheel, blinking his eyes as if he were fighting sleep.

"If you're just going back because I wanted to," Sam said. "Well, you're bigger and older and . . . and I'll do what you think we ought to do. You want to go on to Camp Gualala?"

If necessary, Sam was prepared to repent even more. He'd confess to his stupidity at climbing the

106

redwood after Allan had advised against it. He'd been lucky one of the branches hadn't broken. He'd been lucky he hadn't fallen. *Luck, that's all it was, Allan. And I was scared . . . so scared that I bet I'll never be able to climb again. Honest.*

He ought to really *say* all those things. But he didn't.

"No," Allan said. "Horace is right. We'd get caught sooner or later."

"Something else," Horace said. "Even if it was later instead of sooner, I'd still make a suggestion. You don't have to take it, of course. That's your business. But I advise you to take another look at things at home. Your folks . . . well, they're *your* mother and father . . . they can't be as mean as you think. Mothers and fathers love their children, take care of them. When kids learn that, well, it's usually too late. My suggestion: talk to your folks, tell them why you ran off."

Sam knew Allan was thinking if they didn't know now, they'd never know.

In his own way Allan had tried, perhaps too often, to let their mother and father know that the gulf between them was widening, that they were being deserted even while their mother and father were declaring concern.

Well, if Allan couldn't bridge that gulf, maybe Sam could. Maybe, being the youngest and the most favored, he might succeed where Allan had failed.

The mute reception of Horace's suggestion must have given him the feeling that both boys were seriously considering what he'd said. While Horace leaned closer to the windshield, straining to guide the truck at the edge of the center line, Sam said that maybe, when they got home, their mother and father *would* be so happy to see them that this evening *would* be the time to talk to them.

"Horace," Allan said, "if we come out on week-ends, can we work with you?"

"It's all right with me if it's OK with your folks."

107

"Can we ride the tractor?" Sam said. "And help you fix things?"

"I hardly ever drive the tractor myself anymore. And so far as helping me, well, things have gotten to the point where I could use some good help. Never wanted help before. Always had to do things alone. In fact, no one's been in the house except that inspector. And he's dead."

"We're the only ones who know your secret?" Sam asked.

"That's right. So there's no reason not to let you come. But you've got to swear an oath you'll never tell anyone what I've been doing all these years. You'll never tell what's in the house and the barn. You swear it?"

"I'll never tell," Allan said. "I swear."

"Me, too," Sam said. "I swear."

Sam relaxed. Horace's trust had lifted Allan out of his sadness.

"I forgot," Allan said. "What about Thelma? You said we could bring Thelma."

"You . . . you see . . . you see," Horace said, slapping the steering wheel with the palm of his hand. "That's what happens. You let one person come and that person brings another person and that one brings . . . and pretty soon . . . I don't know . . ."

"Thelma's our friend," Sam said. "If we tell her where we're going and she comes and we ask her not to tell, she won't tell. Allan and her and me . . . we have lots of secrets. We trust each other."

"Thelma will swear the oath, too," Allan said.

"All you talk about is Thelma. I don't know . . ."

"Thelma's been working at our house long as I can remember," Allan said. "She lives in Oakland. When Mom and Dad went away, when we were little, we'd go

108

to Thelma's for the weekend or for whatever time they were gone."

"Well," Horace said, "OK. You like Thelma so much, OK. You can bring her. But no one else."

"No one else," Allan said.

Sam lay back then. Both he and Allan remained silent while Horace described the land they were driving through. He told them how the country had looked when he'd first come to Anders Corners. There had been forests over what were now fields. Pine and cypress mainly, with a few redwoods here and there. Deer were so common that they had to be chased away, like cats or dogs. Foxes hung around the barns and back doors, waiting for a stray chicken. Every week or so someone would shoot a bear that had made a nuisance of itself. You could hear mountain lions at night screaming in the woods, and there must have been a thousand different kinds of birds. You could ride for days in almost any direction and not meet more than one or two families. And fish? The Redwood River was so thick with salmon sometimes that you could wade into the water and catch them with your bare hands.

"Did you ever see a mountain lion?"

"I've seen them and I've shot them. A friend of mine, Luther Goodfellow, he found a den once. Was hauling out the cubs . . . two of them . . . when the mother showed up. He jumped into the Redwood River still holding the two cubs. There was a log and he climbed on, still holding the cubs. They floated maybe ten miles downstream, and when the log got close to shore, Luther jumped off and waded to the bank, the cubs under his arms. There was the mother lion, waiting for him. She'd followed him the whole way. He tossed the cubs on the bank and jumped back in the river."

There were more stories about hunting and trapping

109

and cattle-rustling and stampedes. One story after another, with the final one, about an albino buck with antlers spreading six feet, being completed just as the truck wheezed up Main Street in Anders Corners.

Horace jockeyed the truck back and forth until he had the front wheel against the curb, directly in front of the drugstore. "You can call from there," Horace said. "Good place to wait. Only place in town open today, I guess. Except the bar."

Allan laughed. "I can see Dad's face if we call and tell him we're at a bar in Anders Corners and will he come pick us up."

Horace worked the gearshift into neutral. "OK," he said. "We can get out now." He helped the boys remove their bicycles from the truck bed, and then the three of them stood there, no one willing to be the first to say good-bye.

"Now don't start feeling bad," Horace said. "I'll see you next weekend. If your folks want to bring you, it's fine with me. It's just that . . . well, I wouldn't want . . . you know . . . I don't think they ought to know about what I've been doing in the house and the barn and . . ."

"We won't tell them," Allan said. "And if they bring us, they won't come inside. I promise."

There was no reason to continue standing there. But they did. Allan made the first move, extending his hand to Horace. "See you next Saturday. If it's OK, can we stay overnight?"

"Right," Horace said. "Right as rain."

Sam accepted Horace's hand. Four or five hours ago he'd wanted to run from this man. Now he wished he could stay with him forever. "Good-bye, Horace. And thanks for the ster . . . stereo . . ."

"Stereographoscope. Good-bye, son." The word

110

son acted like an electric switch, stiffening Horace's arm and body. Sam felt the weathered hand grow rigid in his fingers. He saw Horace bring the other hand up, slowly, dreamily, to wipe his leathery cheek. Then, mumbling, the old man slipped his hand from Sam's fingers and felt his way around the truck to the driver's side. The motor coughed and the exhaust pipe rattled and spit out three puffs of choking black smoke. The body of the truck trembled and rocked on the smooth black tires. The motor grew quiet, then roared. The truck leaped away from the curb and staggered up the street.

The boys remained at the curb, leaning on their bikes, until the truck disappeared.

"C'mon," Allan said. "We better call home."

Inside the drugstore a young man standing behind a cash register was using red and blue felt-tipped pens to color a message already outlined on a piece of cardboard: "Regular price $1.00 . . . Sale Price 85¢." A white paper cap, perched precariously on a ball of red hair, had to be constantly repositioned. Chocolate stains formed a thick chain on the left lapel of what had once been a white jacket.

The clerk looked up, nodded, and returned to his work, managing all the while to keep an eye on the mirror above the cash register. Reflected in the mirror, two young girls, the only other customers in the store, were comparing lipsticks, powders, soaps, and perfumes.

The phone booth stood at the far end of the store, near the prescription counter. A blue and red sign sat on an easel on the white formica: "Closed except for emergency."

Allan half closed the door of the booth and inserted a dime. Sam heard the operator ask for the number he was calling. Allan recited their home number. The charge for three minutes, the operator said, would be twenty-five cents. Allan put down the phone and searched his pockets. "You have a quarter?" he asked.

Sam had several pennies, two nickels, and three dimes. He poured the coins into Allan's hand. Allan selected the appropriate coins from Sam's and his own collection, and he waited.

Leaning against the booth, Sam watched the two young girls continue their performance at the cosmetics counter. The clerk at the cash register interrupted his observation in the mirror to fill in the letter *P* with a felt-tipped pen.

Sam leaned into the phone booth. "What's happening?"

"Busy. Operator said to wait, and she'll keep trying."

Sam was relieved that Allan and not he was calling home. If he called, he'd probably start bawling the instant he heard his mother's voice. Not Allan. Allan stood there as cool as if he were calling a radio station for the score of a ball game.

For a moment today . . . that moment he'd climbed past Allan on the redwood . . . Sam had sensed that things had changed, that he'd changed things. It would all be different now . . . from now on. He could not possibly ever be Allan's *little* brother anymore. But despite the inevitability of that change, of Sam's new role, here was Allan assuming the responsibility for calling their parents. And here was Sam relieved that it was Allan, cool and calm, who was calling. Sam had been terrified, when they'd moved toward the phone booth, that Allan would automatically expect him to call. But Allan was calling. Sam was just as terrified now when he thought of the impending trip home, and even more terrified of the possibilities that could arise during the remainder of the evening. They were sure to be examined and cross-examined.

As painful and challenging as it was to be a little brother, the demands to be simply a brother could be even more challenging. He had found the courage to grab at that first spike in the redwood tree and pull himself toward the second one and then to haul his body through branch after branch until the wind had whipped his apprehension into joy into thrill into ecstasy. Would he now find the courage with such ease and such ecstasy when he faced his mother and father and sought to answer the inevitable questions? Or would he take refuge, as he always had before, in their faith in his innocence? Would he, as he always had before, let Allan bear the burden of guilt as well as of explanation?

"Mom? . . . Hi, it's Allan . . . yeah . . . well, don't cry. . . . Sure I'm OK. . . . Sure he is, he's right here beside me. . . . We're at . . ." Allan shook his head and sighed. "She's getting Dad," he said. "Hi, Dad. . . . Yeah, we're OK. . . . We just decided to go on a . . . well, a sort of exploration, on our bikes. . . . We're at Anders Corners. Yeah, on our bikes. We're at the drugstore. It's right on Main Street, across from a Texaco station. Yeah, that's right. A bus bench right outside. Right. In an hour. We'll be waiting on the bench in an hour."

Allan hung the phone on its hook, and he stepped out of the booth.

"Was he mad?" Sam asked.

"Nah. He was happy. Cracked all kinds of jokes. What do you think?"

"He was mad."

"Pretended not to be, but he was. I could tell. They're driving right over to pick us up. Be here in an hour. Dad knows where Anders Corners is and where

113

the drugstore is. He's been here. How much do you have left?"

Sam counted his money. "Two dollars. And the change I gave you for the call."

"I've got two dollars and ... well, let's have a hamburger."

"Hey, yeah. And a milk shake."

"And the condemned men," Allan said, "ate a hearty meal."

The clerk at the cash register said he was sorry, but he didn't have hot sandwiches on Sunday. There were cold sandwiches in the refrigerator left over from Saturday. Did they want one of those?

Allan had a ham sandwich and Sam had a salami and cheese. They both ordered milk shakes, and while the clerk prepared them, he confided to them that this had been just about the quietest Sunday on record. Except for those two chicks messing up the lipstick (and now Sam and Allan), there hadn't been but three customers all day. There'd been a woman in for a hot-water bottle and an old man for a box of corn plasters and a man who'd bought a five-pound box of chocolates. "Wanted it gift-wrapped," the clerk said, shaking his head in disbelief. "On Sunday. Well, I gave him a red ribbon, and he wrapped it all around the box and took it like that, with a card he drew a red heart on. Borrowed my pen. Came back and drew an arrow through the heart. He left and came again. You know what for? To print initials inside the heart. Where you from? You ain't from around here. You friends of old Hoss Butright?"

"Sort of," Sam said. "Why? How'd you know?"

"Saw him get your bikes off his truck. You been out at the dump?"

Sam started to say yes, but Allan nudged him. The clerk grinned. "What's wrong with that? I don't care if

114

you've been at the dump. What's so secret about being at the dump?"

"Nothing's secret," Sam said. He didn't like the clerk, who reminded him too much of Teddy Rogers. Teddy was always trying, in vain, to get him to fight. Tomorrow, he decided, Teddy Rogers was going to be surprised.

"How'd you get to know him? You're not from around here, and Hoss doesn't have any friends. You relatives?"

"He's a friend of our dad's," Allan said. "In fact, our dad's coming to pick us up."

"That right? Where you from?"

"Walnut Creek," Allan said, moving his right foot so he might tap a signal to Sam. But Sam wasn't sure what message was being signaled. Was he supposed to let Allan do all the talking? Or was he just being prepared to confirm additional lies? He didn't know, but he was willing to let Allan fix the rules.

"Walnut Creek, huh? That's pretty far to come on a bike. How'd you get across the freeway? The freeway's the only way from Walnut Creek to Anders Corners."

"We rode the freeway."

"On your bikes?"

"You know the fine for riding bikes on a freeway? A hundred dollars. And there are cops patrolling all the time."

"They didn't catch us."

The clerk was impressed. He made a nut sundae for himself and leaned on the counter while he ate it. "You inside old Butright's shack?"

Allan pretended he hadn't heard. He appeared to be more interested in the ice cream plugging his straw.

"Were you?" the clerk asked, speaking directly to Sam.

Sam said, "Yes." When Allan's heel stomped on his foot, he simply withdrew his foot and asked, "Why do you want to know?"

The clerk laughed. "I was out there once with some buddies. He's crazy, you know that? He ought to be put away. He's going to be, too. Crazy."

"You one of the gang he chased off?"

The clerk looked as if he now considered *Sam* to be crazy. "Chased off? He tell you he chased us off? Ha! He didn't chase us off. He's flipped. He doesn't know . . ."

"He shot firecrackers at you," Sam said. "And you all ran."

"He tell you that?"

"Yeah, and I believe him."

The clerk's face turned red, and he busied himself with a spot on the counter, wiping it with a wet gray rag. "Well," he said, "I guess we did run." He stepped back and leaned against the ice-cream freezer. "About ten of us. He sure surprised us. He told you the truth. We got out of there so fast . . ." His laughter swept whipped cream from his sundae onto the counter, and he collected the cream in his rag, still laughing. "You know, he never called the cops. He must be about a hundred years old, but he's cool. Wonder where he'll go next." The clerk nodded at the black box resting on the stool next to Sam. "What's in the box? Some of his rockets?"

"An atom bomb," Allan said. He climbed off his stool. "Come on, Sam. We better get out on the bench."

The clerk rang up the sale, gave them their change, and then, while they were walking toward the front door, called after them, "You can't kid me. You couldn't have come the whole way on the freeway. Not from Walnut Creek."

They sat on the bench, one on each side of the black box containing the stereographoscope and the slides.

116

Allan was angry. Sam knew it without looking at him.

"What's wrong?" Sam said.

"I told you not to say anything."

"You did not."

"I signaled you. With my elbow and my foot. What do you think I was trying to do?"

"How was I to know? I can't read your mind. Anyway, why shouldn't I talk if I feel like it? You can't tell me when to talk and when not to."

There it was: one more face of the courage discovered today.

Allan reached out and pushed Sam's leg with his foot. "You watch. I bet you spill everything. I bet you end up telling them where we were, what Horace has in his house . . . everything. And you swore an oath."

"I can keep a secret as good as you can."

"Like you kept our secret in there? You told him everything."

"I did not. I didn't tell him anything. I told him what he already knew."

"Wait and see. You'll be bawling and promising you'll never go out again without asking, you'll never run away again, won't Mommy and Daddy forgive you, do Mommy and Daddy still love you and . . ."

Sam, retaliating, kicked Allan's foot harder than he'd been kicked. Allan, in response, punched him on the shoulder, and Sam, in response to that, punched Allan even harder. They fell together, wrestling, each trying to throw the other to the ground. Sam was younger, but he was also forty pounds heavier. Balancing that was Allan's experience. He'd fought half of the boys in his class and, in the process, had learned how to use his fists and body. Tall and slim, he was already smoothly muscled. When they roughhoused at home, for fun, Allan, faster and more aggressive, was always able to feint Sam

117

out of position and trip him to the ground. But now Sam, who'd never fought in anger with anyone, was fighting back . . . and growling and snarling like an animal.

He knew that by keeping Allan close, it would be more difficult for Allan to feint him off his feet. With his left arm hugging the slim, straining body, he kept punching his right fist at Allan's face and head. A solid punch on his own nose brought tears to Sam's eyes and a louder series of growls and snarls. With a bellow of outrage, he lifted Allan off the ground and slammed him down on the bench. Allan's head struck with a dull thud, and his body went limp in Sam's arms.

Sam stepped back, expecting Allan to leap up. He did not. He remained lying on the bench, silent, his face white, one arm up over the black box.

"Allan?"

Allan did not move.

"Come on, Allan. You're just playing. Allan . . . are you really hurt, Allan?"

No response.

Sam shook his brother's shoulder. After several groans Allan's head moved. He tried to focus his eyes, but they remained glazed. He sat up, halfway, and then, blinking and shaking his head, he rubbed behind his right ear. "What happened?"

"We were wrestling. You hit your head on the bench."

"I did?"

"Yeah. You OK, Al?"

"I think so. I must have knocked myself out."

"You did. I . . . whew! . . . I thought you were dead."

"I'm not dead." They both giggled. Sam sat down beside his brother, his hands trembling. "What did happen?" Allan asked.

"I told you. We were fighting and you hit . . ."

"What were we fighting about?"

"I can't remember."

"You do so. I was saying you'll tell Mom and Dad everything. Wow! I have a goose egg. Feel."

Sam placed his still quivering hand at the base of Allan's skull, behind the ear. The lump was impressive, all right.

"I'm sorry, Al."

"Well, I yelled at you. I started it."

"Aw, you didn't exactly yell."

"Hey . . . you're getting strong. I bet if you wanted to, you could take Teddy Rogers or Billy Gallagher or Fudge or any of those guys."

A mix of pride and pleasure shot through Sam's chest. He sat back on the bench and kicked his feet and watched the road, hoping his dad would hurry so he might prove to both Allan and himself that the courage with which he'd been so infected today had not just been the courage to climb trees or to fight.

Allan kept rubbing the bump on his head. Without warning he reached over and pushed, rather than punched, Sam's shoulder. He was grinning. Sam, also grinning, did not respond.

"I was really out," Allan said. "I really was. You sure you didn't hit me?"

Sam giggled and walked out into the street. Where were they? Why weren't they here? What in the hell was taking them so long? He tested the words aloud. "What in the hell's taking them so long?"

Allan *had* to be impressed. *He* was.

Chapter 8

Before the green station wagon rolled to a stop at the curb, Mrs. Collins had her door open and was rushing to the bus bench. She embraced Sam and then Allan and then Sam again. Mr. Collins opened the rear of the station wagon to slide the two bicycles inside. When Allan offered to help him, he slammed the door closed and walked, chin out, scowling, toward the front seat. "Just get the hell in the car."

Both boys recognized the same barely stifled anger they'd witnessed twice in the last month.

Once, the first time, they'd accompanied their father to Richmond, where Collins Construction Company was building the largest parking tower in the entire bay area. Two workers had arrived on the job drunk, had ruined several thousand dollars' worth of heavy equipment, and had almost killed a foreman. When Mr. Collins had warned the two men to leave and they'd ignored him, he'd thrown both men, bodily, from a platform ten feet high.

After paying the hospital bills Mr. Collins insisted the workers receive disability pay.

The second time was two weeks ago, when a professor from the university in Berkeley was canvassing every house in Orchid, soliciting names for a petition that protested United States' involvement in the Vietnam war. Mr. Collins had listened as the professor introduced himself, he'd listened to the reading of two sentences from the heading of the petition, and then he'd grabbed the professor by his coat lapels and hustled him through the gate, warning the unprotesting scholar about his fate should he ever again show his face in the Collins house or on this street or in the town of Orchid.

Sam managed to follow Allan into the back seat without damaging the black box containing his gift from Horace.

Once they were all in the car, Mrs. Collins said something about her little family being together again. She wiped her eyes and blew her nose.

"Now," Mr. Collins said, as he pulled the Oldsmobile away from the curb, "I want a complete accounting. You've just about driven your mother out of her mind. Why did you do this?"

Sam started to answer, but Allan replied before the last word was out of his father's mouth. "We just decided to go for an all-day ride."

"You just decided? Without permission? Without even telling anyone? Do you realize that I had to cancel today's picnic? I had to call *every*one and cancel it. Do you realize I've spent the entire afternoon at the police station?"

"Harry," Mrs. Collins said, "please." She touched his arm. "Maybe we ought to talk about all this tomorrow. The boys are back and they're safe. That's what matters."

"Sure that's what matters. And I'm glad they're

121

back, too. But this . . . this doing whatever they damn well please, that's got to stop and stop *now*. Do you two realize," Mr. Collins said, peering into the rear-view mirror, "your mother's been on the phone all day, calling your friends and everyone she could think of, including Thelma? I had to talk to reporters at the police station and . . ."

"Reporters?" Mrs. Collins said. "You didn't tell me . . ."

"Of course I didn't tell you. You were scared enough already."

"But why would there be reporters?"

"Because there could have been a kidnap story for them, that's why."

"Kidnappers," Sam said, "wouldn't have let us take our bikes."

Normally such a demonstration of Sam's deductive powers would have brought a wink of recognition, an exchange of hushed congratulations between mother and father. But not today. Today that demonstration kindled a fury that seemed to have been lying in wait for the appropriate spark. "Sam, you keep quiet. You keep quiet and you stay quiet. Allan, you organized this. *You* answer my questions."

Sam's voice, weak and timid, brought the faces of both mother and father about. "It was both of us."

They were on the freeway, heading toward the Richmond Bridge. They settled in the center lane, traveling well over seventy miles an hour. Mr. Collins spoke to the reflection of Sam in his mirror. "OK, you want to play the big shot. What the hell's in that box you're hiding?"

"I'm not hiding anything," Sam said, trying to squeeze the box to the floor.

"Sam," Mrs. Collins said, "let me have it."

122

"Mom, it's not anything. It's a present. Someone gave it to me."

"Sam! You do as you're told! Give that box to your mother!"

Sam eased the box over the top of the seat into his mother's lap.

"What is it?" Mr. Collins asked.

Mrs. Collins removed the lid. "It's an old-fashioned . . . I forget what you call it."

"It's an old stereoscope. Look at that thing. Why, it's . . . it's a museum piece. And all those slides. Where'd you get that, Sam? That's not a cheap toy from a drugstore. Where'd you get it?"

"I found it."

"Found it?" Mrs. Collins said, her scowl and O-shaped mouth conveying her suspicions.

Mr. Collins, still speaking into the mirror, said, "You just told me it was a present. Allan, where'd Sam get that?"

"Like he said, it was a present."

Mr. Collins guided the station wagon off the road and onto the shoulder. The rear wheels skidded in the gravel. He pulled on the brake and twisted his body on the seat into a half-kneeling, half-sitting position. "Where did that thing come from? Is it stolen? Did you steal it, Sam?"

Sam's voice grew sharper and stronger with each word. "Why do you say I stole it? Why couldn't someone give it to me?"

"Someone would not just *give* something as valuable as that is, as a gift, to you. Now you better tell me where you got it."

"I told you. I found it, and the man who owned it gave it to me."

"What man? Where?"

Sam shook his head and slid down in the seat. Mrs. Collins ordered him to sit up straight. "Answer your father. Where did this come from?"

Sam struggled to keep from sobbing and then tried to muffle the sounds behind his arms.

His mother's quiet, almost tender interrogation did little to soothe him. "You didn't steal it, did you, Sam? If you did, you just say so and we can take it back. We can explain to whoever . . ."

"I didn't steal it!" Sam screamed, thrusting his face to within an inch of his mother's face and then falling back as his father . . . rage draining his face of all color . . . leaned over the back of the seat, his arm raised.

Mrs. Collins caught his wrist. "No, Harry. Don't. That won't help."

Mr. Collins settled back in his seat. He put the car in gear and moved back onto the freeway. "OK, gentlemen. It looks like we have a long, rough evening ahead of us."

Sam burrowed down into the upholstery. Allan inched his hand along the seat until his fingers touched Sam's leg. He clenched his fist, in a sign of strength, and winked. Then Allan put a finger to his lips and after that he clenched both hands together and shook them in a gesture of victory.

For the rest of the ride home no one said a word. Allan and Sam sat far apart in the back seat, no longer signaling each other, and Mr. and Mrs. Collins sat in the front seat, quiet, sullen, staring at the lights of the oncoming traffic. Once, when Mr. Collins cut out into traffic to pass a Volkswagen bus loaded with long-haired youths and then cut in front of the bus, sharply, Mrs. Collins gasped and started to complain but then, apparently, changed her mind.

After the electric eye clicked and the garage door opened and Mr. Collins drove the station wagon inside,

124

he remained sitting there, his hands clasped over the steering wheel. Mrs. Collins got out and opened the back door for the boys. "You two go on inside. Take a shower, get into your pajamas, and then come have your supper. Go on."

"What about my . . . ?"

"Samuel Patrick Collins, you do as you're told."

They went into the house, through the kitchen and down the corridor, the dark oak floors gleaming on either side of the white wool carpet. In his room, while taking off his clothes, Sam sat on the floor and leaned back against the footboard of his bed. From where he sat he could see the backyard. In the crisp, pale moonlight his father stood at the edge of the pool, staring down into the water.

Allan sat on his bed in his room for just a moment. He watched the silhouette of the tree against the wall, and then he went to the window and opened it. From the tree came the sounds of dry leaves rustling, birds settling down for the night, limbs and branches scraping each other, complaining to the wind and to him. He removed his clothes and took a fast shower. After he dried himself he put on his favorite flannel pajamas and his robe. When he went down the hall to Sam's room, Sam, still dressed, was sitting on the floor. "You better hurry," Allan said. "Dad's waiting."

"He's out by the pool," Sam said.

Allan walked to the window. "He looks like he's ready to jump in."

"I've never seen him so mad. He was ready to hit me."

"Yeah. I knew he'd be mad, but I never thought he'd be like that. Mom, too."

"But why, Allan? Why? What did we do that was so wrong?"

"We ran away. Without asking permission."

125

"But how can you run away if you ask permission? And anyway, we're back." Sam, by now, had removed both shoes. He took off a sock and threw it against the wall. "I don't like it like this. They're so mean. Like . . . how can I convince them I didn't steal that stereo . . . ster . . ."

"Stereographoscope."

"They're sure I stole it. They *know*." Allan left the window and sat on Sam's bed. "Dad's coming in the house. You better hurry."

"Why are they so sure? Why don't they believe me? Even if I were lying, they ought to trust me. They always have."

"Well, they won't from now on." Allan stood in the shadows near the closet and continued watching their father. "You aren't going to tell, are you?" he said.

"Tell?"

"On Horace."

"No. We promised."

"That's right. Just remember; no matter *what*, we won't tell."

"No matter what."

Mrs. Collins's voice came from the kitchen. "You boys ready yet?"

Sam rushed into the bathroom, shedding clothes as he ran. Above the noise inside the shower stall, Allan replied that they'd be out in a minute.

Soaped and somewhat rinsed, dripping water beneath his towel, Sam returned to his bedroom to find Allan lying on his bed, staring at the ceiling.

Sam's pajama bottoms went on fairly easily, but he had to struggle . . . turning and tugging and grunting . . . to pull the top over his head and down across his wet shoulders and back. "We better go, Allan." He grabbed his orange terry-cloth robe and fought his feet into his

126

slippers. Allan continued to lie on the bed, staring at the ceiling.

"Al?"

"Hm?"

"We better go in."

"Remember our promise."

"I'll remember."

When they entered the kitchen, on their way to the living room, Sam, leading the way, suddenly rushed forward. "Thelma!"

Thelma was standing at the long maple-topped counter. Instead of her usual white uniform, she wore a black dress and high-heeled shoes. She'd never worn jewelry before, but she was wearing jewelry tonight, long silver hoop earrings and a pearl necklace. Sam fell into her arms, burrowing his face into the softness of her body. Allan, more reticent but no less delighted, stood at her side, leaning against her, accepting an embrace from her free arm and repeating, "Hi, Thelma . . . hi, Thelma . . ." He finally reached up one hand to touch her arm.

"How long have you been here?" Sam asked.

"About ten minutes. Now where you two been? Running off like that, scaring your momma and poppa. Shame on you."

"We had fun," Sam said.

Allan stepped back, his eyes bright. "Will you come with us next Sunday? We asked and he said we could bring you. Just you, no one else."

"Bring me where? Who's this *he* says you can bring me? What you two talking about?" She laughed. "You better get in that living room. They sitting there, that conversation pit, waiting. Like Romans watching them lions chomping Christians. I'll tell you. You go in there, don't sit down by the fire, the bottom that pit. You sit on top, the top step. Now you go on in. I'm fixing up some food for you. Called a cab and it's gonna be here in a little while. So you go on, get it over with."

"But will you come?" Allan persisted. "Will you? Please. His name's Horace and he has all these old things . . ."

"We'll talk about that tomorrow. Tonight you better go in there and settle things with your momma and poppa. Go on, go on now, 'fore I'm chased on home."

Sam backed off, freeing Thelma with great reluctance. He led the way out of the kitchen, down the hall, through the door, and into the living room. He marched to the top step of the conversation pit and sat down. Allan, trailing behind, sat several feet away from him at first and then moved close, until their bodies almost touched.

Mr. Collins had built one of his famous fires and was engaged now in shifting logs back and forth.

"It's late," Mrs. Collins said. "Thelma will have some food ready for you in a little while. In the meantime . . ."

"In the meantime," Mr. Collins said, "we better talk."

"Dear, you said you'd let me handle this."

Mr. Collins jabbed at one of the logs with the tip of the iron poker, sending sparks through the firebox and up the chimney.

Thelma came in then, carrying a tray containing sandwiches and glasses and a pitcher of milk. She set the tray on the second step down, in front of the boys.

"Thelma, I'm sorry I didn't call you," Mrs. Collins said. "I should have called you as soon as the boys phoned, so you wouldn't have to make the trip, but I was so . . . I just forgot."

"Don't think nothing of it," Thelma said. "You or Mr. Collins want anything 'fore I leave?"

128

"No, thanks," Mrs. Collins said, after Mr. Collins shook his head. Mrs. Collins reached into a pocket of her dress and withdrew a folded bill. "This is for both cabs. And something extra. And thank you again. I don't know what we'd all do without you."

"Nothing," Thelma said. "Nothing at all. You mind I just sit right here till that cab comes?"

Mrs. Collins did not reply. Thelma sat in the chair next to the front door. Mr. Collins looked as though he was going to ask her to wait somewhere else, in the kitchen or outside, but then, distracted by a falling log, he concentrated on his fire.

Sam's appetite was not impaired. He ate his first sandwich and was picking up a second one before Allan swallowed his first bite. Mr. Collins, as he himself would have said, took the bull by the horns. "Your mother and I have been talking about what you did . . ."

"Dear . . ."

"We've decided to get everything out in the open to-night."

"Dear, we agreed that I'd handle this. You're too angry. You admitted that yourself."

"Well, get started. We've been home for more than an hour, and they haven't told us anything."

Mrs. Collins moved to the top step, across the curve from Sam and Allan. She carried her bourbon and soda with her. Mr. Collins's glass of iced Scotch sat on the walnut mantel. He took a drink from the glass now and shook his head.

"Sam," Mrs. Collins said, "I'm asking you first because you're the youngest and you're usually asked things last." Mr. Collins groaned and kneeled before the flames, waiting to reconstruct his fire if it should threaten collapse. "Why did you run away?"

Sam shrugged. "I don't know. I guess I just sort of wanted some adventure."

"Do you know what I had planned for today?" Mr. Collins snapped, bracing his hands on his hips.

"Well, a picnic, I guess . . ."

"We were going, it so happens, near where I picked you up. I'm going to build a marina near there, for the county. I won the contract. Twenty contractors from all over the state bid the job, and I won it. Me, Harry Collins, who didn't have but one truck to my name ten years ago. Biggest job I've ever had. Could lead to jobs even bigger. I'm moving equipment in next week, to level the place, get it set for surveys. I wanted us all to see it now, take pictures of it now. Before and after pictures. That's where we were going to have our picnic today. But we couldn't go. We had to stay here . . . the whole day . . . worrying about you two."

"Allan," Mrs. Collins said, "do you have anything to say?"

"No."

Mr. Collins had lifted his glass of Scotch for another drink, but at Allan's single-word response he slammed the glass down on the mantel. "Damn it all, you must have *some*thing to say. Can't you talk? You're reading all the time. You read words, can't you speak them?"

Allan was more concerned with the crust of his half-eaten sandwich than with his father's questions.

"Harry," Mrs. Collins said, her voice growing more frail with each appeal, "I think we're being too hard on them. They ran away. But they're back and . . ."

"Too *hard?* We're being too soft. And that, by God, is the whole problem. But no more. I've decided . . ."

"What I mean is . . . well, maybe we should start all over. The boys are back, they're safe, let's just pretend it didn't happen. Let's say that starting now we'll all be better people."

"My God, your children run away, they foul up my whole Sunday . . ."

130

"*Our* Sunday, dear."

". . . they scare you to death, and you say, 'Let's pretend it didn't happen.' Those kids have to realize they did something *wrong.* If they aren't punished, they'll think they can just take off any time they damn well please."

"I don't think punishment will . . ."

"How do you know what punishment will do? Have you ever punished them? For anything? Why not give them a reward? Here." Mr. Collins rammed his hand into his pocket and pulled out a fistful of five and ten and one dollar bills. He threw the money on the coffee table. "Here. Here's a reward for running away, for fouling up my Sunday, for scaring your mother to death. Next time you'll get twice as much. Does that make you happy, Gladys?"

"You know," and Mrs. Collins's deep breath hovered at the edge of a sob, "you know that's not what I mean."

"Well, what the hell do you mean? Speak up. Say it. Maybe that's the problem. I've let you raise the kids, I've let you discipline them. I only go out and work a twelve-, fourteen-hour day six, seven days a week bringing home the bacon. And I bring home one hell of a lot of bacon, I might add. It's obvious now I should have stepped in sooner, I should have laid down the law a damn sight harder. But from here on . . ."

Mrs. Collins's hands came up over her eyes. "Don't talk to me like that. Please don't. Not now. Not today. Not in front of the boys. I'm tired. I'm so pleased they're back and they're safe and . . ."

Mr. Collins made a feeble pass at one of the logs. Then he whirled and pointed a finger at Allan. "You ever taken drugs?"

"No."

"Are you lying to me?"

131

"No. I'm telling the truth."

"I know your buddies take drugs at school. The Emerson kids got caught right on the playground selling drugs. Now you tell me the truth. Have you? Do you smoke the stuff . . . marijuana . . . LSD . . . that stuff?"

"No."

"Sam, is he telling me the truth?"

"He's telling the truth. But you don't believe him. Why? Why didn't you ask me if I use drugs? You asked Allan but not me. Why?"

Mr. Collins's stiff legs carried him, slowly, to where Sam sat. His anguish was too painfully apparent in his barely audible question. "Sam . . . are you telling me that *you* take drugs? *You?*

"No."

Mr. Collins let the meaning of Sam's reply sink in. He pressed his hands to his temples, as if that would clarify a confusion in his mind. "But you just said . . ." He opened his mouth and closed it and opened it again. "Why did you make me think you did?"

"I didn't."

With a thrust of his arm, Mr. Collins swept the money from the coffee table to the floor. "Don't you play games with me. You're getting just like Allan. You're getting too damned smart for your own good."

"I'm not playing games."

"I know what's responsible for this. That TV. Those riots. In color. Those bombers, those interviews with those bombers. That scum, Jerry Rubin, right on TV. 'Kill your mother and father.' That's what he said. Right on TV. In color. So you wanted adventure, huh? You think it's an adventure to be a revolutionary, is that it?"

"A revolutionary?" Sam said. "Who's a revolutionary?"

But his father ignored the question. "I'll tell you something. You two have had it too easy. Anything you

132

wanted, whenever you wanted it, you got it. Well, no more. You're going to go without things. The first thing that goes is that damned TV. You're going to work for your allowances. And I mean *work*, like I had to."

"Dear, please. For God's sake, stop! Enough. I can't stand it any more."

"You better learn to stand it, Gladys, because things are going to be different around here. Starting now . . . this minute. I want to know where you kids were all day and where you got that stereoscope. Either one of you."

Sam put down the uneaten portion of his third sandwich. He wiped the mayonnaise from all ten fingers, separately, one very slowly after the other. Allan's lips were quivering, but he remained silent.

Mr. Collins said something that Sam could not hear. It sounded like "All right, that's it," or, "All right, let's see it." Then he unbuckled his belt and whipped it out of the loops in his trousers. Mrs. Collins made a gesture of protest and then covered her eyes.

"Allan," Mr. Collins said. "Stand up."

"Mr. Collins, I do not think you ought to do this."

Everyone . . . Sam, Allan, Mrs. Collins, Mr. Collins . . . everyone turned toward the voice that had come from the doorway. Thelma sat straight in the chair, her hands folded over the purse lying in her broad lap.

"Mr. Collins, I've knowed you a long time. You are not a cruel man. Mrs. Collins and me, we talked some about you bein' whipped when you was a boy and you swearin' you never lay a hand on your boys. I do not think you gain anything now, Mr. Collins, you start whippin' them boys now. You better think up some other ways to get them talkin' to you. Layin' a belt to a child, them days are gone, Mr. Collins. You don't need no education to know them days are gone. Your boys, Allan and Sammy, they are good boys, Mr. Collins. They . . ."

"I didn't ask for your advice, Thelma."

133

"You never ask me for anythin'," Thelma said. "Advice or nothin' else. And I never ask you for anythin', leastwise not anythin' I don't earn. And earn the hard way. I'm sayin' . . ."

"Have you been pouring your black-power poison into these boys' heads?"

"Mr. Collins, you go right ahead, blame me or blame Mrs. Collins or blame TV or, like I heard you many a time, blame that university there in Berkeley, but I don't hear you blamin' yourself. Black-power poison, Mr. . . . ?"

Mrs. Collins walked up the steps of the conversation pit to sit beside Thelma. "Don't say any more, Thelma. Please. We're all too emotional. We'll say things we don't mean and then . . ."

"You don't have to worry, Mrs. Collins. I never say somethin' I don't mean."

"Say something I don't mean?" Mr. Collins said. "All right, I'll say something I mean."

"Harry!"

"I've noticed, Thelma, ever since that Watts riot you've been different."

"That's right, that's sure enough right. And I noticed, Mr. Collins, ever since that Watts riot, as you call it, you been the same. Now who's that do more damage to? You or me? Or them two children? Mr. Collins, my children, they're my hope. Your children better be your hope. If they ain't, you got nothin' left, Mr. Collins. Nothin'."

Mrs. Collins, with an arm around Thelma's shoulders, walked her to the door, where they talked for a moment. Then Thelma opened the door. "Sammy and Allan, you boys take care. Rebecca or Ralph was here, they'd put their fists up and they'd say, 'Right on!' Like this." She lifted her clenched fist. "So I'll say it for them." And with that Thelma was gone.

Mr. Collins, his belt hanging like a stripe down the

134

side of his trousers, pointed to the coffee table. "Allan, drop your pajamas and bend over that table."

Mrs. Collins, leaning against the door she'd just closed, pleaded with her husband. "Harry, I can't watch you do this terrible . . ."

"Then don't watch. Go in your bedroom and close the door."

"Harry Collins, it is not *my* bedroom, it's *our* bedroom. This is not *my* house, it is *our* house. Those two boys are not just *your* children, they are also *my* children . . ."

Mr. Collins waivered, but he did not replace his belt. Then he turned away from his wife with a wave of contempt.

"Allan, one more chance. Where were you today? Who gave you that thing in the box? Either of you answer those two questions, we'll call it quits. Does that suit you, Gladys?"

"Boys, answer your father. Please do."

Sam turned to Allan, but Allan continued staring at the floor. He remained silent, as if his father's question did not deserve the courtesy of an answer.

"All right," Mr. Collins said. "Over the table."

Allan stood up, snapped the front of his pajamas loose and let the pajamas fall to the floor. He went to the coffee table, pulled up his robe to expose his buttocks, and lay across the table.

Mrs. Collins ran down the hall. Her weeping could be heard even after she closed the door of her bedroom.

The leather belt went up, to dangle from Mr. Collins's shoulder.

Sam's eyes shifted from the belt to the white tight face of Allan to the white agonized face of his father to Allan's twitching white buttocks to his father's clenched teeth and narrowed, almost closed eyes. "No . . . don't . . . I'll tell . . . I'll tell . . ."

135

Sam raised his face from the carpet. Allan's head was turned, his eyes flashing in anger. "You promised," he said. Then he closed his eyes and waited for the belt to strike.

But Mr. Collins's arm was lowered. His darkly tanned face had grown a pale, ashen gray, but the mouth was no longer tight, the jaw muscles no longer twitching.

"Horace Butright," Sam said. "At the dump. We were there all day. He gave me the stereo . . . stereo . . ."

"Horace Butright? The dump? The dump at Anders Corners?"

"An old man . . . he runs the dump. We ate there and we saw all the things he has and . . ."

"That tramp? That old tramp?" Mr. Collins sputtered. "That bum? What do you mean you ate there? What do you . . . you saw all the things he has?" He tossed his belt on the floor, in front of the fireplace. He climbed the four steps of the conversation pit and, at the entry to the hall that led to the bedrooms, he called Mrs. Collins. "Gladys, you better come out here. You better hear where your boys were today."

Mr. Collins returned to the fireplace, picking up his belt and slipping it back through the loops in his trousers. Mrs. Collins's slippers tap-tapped down the hall.

Allan pulled on his pajama bottoms, snapped them closed, and sat on the top step. A faint smear of perspiration lay on his forehead and upper lip, but there was neither apology nor regret in his eyes. He did not look at Sam.

Mr. Collins arranged a pillow for his wife. When she sat . . . her cheeks wet, her eyes puffy . . . she pushed the pillow aside.

"Well," Mr. Collins said, "maybe you two better go on to bed. I want to talk to your mother."

Sam shuffled down the hallway behind Allan, who went into his room and closed the door. In his own room,

136

Sam crawled under the blankets and pulled them up to his nose. Over the rim of the blankets his eyes sought out familiar patterns in the shadows. Eventually he found the outlines of the P-47 Thunderbolt he'd built last summer. Suspended from the ceiling near the window, it dipped and revolved in the breeze that slipped beneath the door. He stared until his eyes ached, and then he rode the plane into a troubled sleep.

And Allan, standing at the open window in his room, looked up into the depths of the old oak, listening for some comforting sounds. But the birds were strangely silent and the limbs motionless. He did not know how long he stood there, but eventually the wind rose to shuffle the leaves, to scrape branch against branch, to stir faint sounds of protest from one restless bird. Then he went to bed. As he drifted into sleep, his eyes caught Sam's *U.S.S. Kennedy* plowing her way across the ocean that covered his desk.

Chapter 9

"Did you hear the question, Allan? Allan . . . you're not paying attention."

Mrs. Weyand repeated the question, but Allan continued staring out of the window. Teddy Rogers called out, "Hey, Al, they come down on you last night?" Mrs. Weyand told Teddy to report to the principal's office. She deserted Allan, turning to Penny Robertson for the answer.

Allan did not care about Mrs. Weyand being irritated or Teddy Rogers being punished. He did not care about the school. Neither Mrs. Weyand nor Teddy Rogers knew it, but he wasn't even in the school. He was walking down Moonglow to the freeway, hitching a ride to Anders Corners, walking and hitching along the asphalt road to the dump.

He walked alone, without Sam. Not because he was angry, he wasn't . . . not any more at least. Sam was still young, still trusting enough to resist cutting ties. It was time he found his own strength to fight his own battles.

Long after his mother had tucked the blankets around his chin last night and assured him that everything would be fine, and long after she'd turned off the light, Allan had lain awake in bed. Everything was not going to be fine. They would never understand what had happened, and neither he nor Sam would ever be able to tell them. Now they were beyond knowing each other, beyond talking to each other. He might, for a few more years, continue living here, continue sitting at the same table, even continue conversations. But in five or six or seven years he would be gone. He would not say good-bye. He would not pack any clothes. He would open the door and walk out. He would not even look back.

When his father had so promptly and casually judged him responsible for their flight from home, Allan had not considered the fact that his father had spoken the truth. Whether it was true or false didn't matter. What mattered was the speed and certainty with which blame was allotted. No uncertainty, no discussion, no regrets. And no sympathy.

He'd not been surprised when Sam had broken down and admitted that they'd been to the County Dump, that they'd stayed with Horace, that Horace had given him the stereographoscope. He'd predicted that Sam would go running to them weeping and asking forgiveness. Secretly, he'd been hoping his prediction would prove wrong.

Would he have rushed to save Sam from being beaten with the belt? No, not if it had meant betraying Horace. And so he was neither flattered nor impressed by the fact that, for Sam, he was more important than Horace.

What would he, Allan, do even if he ran to Horace by himself? Horace had asked for their trust, and they had offered it. Could he stay with Horace and pretend to him that their friendship was still pure, that their trust in each other was still intact? No. So that, too, was at an end.

They would not see Horace again. Almost certainly they would never see Thelma again.

A crumpled brown paper bag tumbling across the black alphalt playground caught Allan's attention.

At the edge of the playground, on the other side of the fence, the brown grass rippled up to distant hills. California oaks, their trunks twisted and gnarled, dipped into and swept up out of the rippling grass. When Horace's redwood had been fifty or a hundred years old, these oaks had been seedlings. Allan had climbed along the limbs of those oaks many times. After he left Orchid, would Sam try to climb them? And after the oaks, would he try the acacia behind the ballfield? And the eucalyptus trees near Lake Temescal?

No. Sam would probably never climb a tree again. His courage yesterday just had to have been an accident. If they were at the dump right now, Sam would probably stand at the base of the redwood, making excuses about his leg hurting or his hand aching or his eyes burning. While Allan scurried up the tree, Sam would find something more challenging inside the house.

Would Sam, after Allan left, no longer be disturbed by the boredom and resentment that had driven them both down the driveway yesterday? Would Sam eventually decide that he had been victimized by no one except his brother?

"Allan."

"Yes, ma'am."

Mrs. Weyand's hand touched his shoulder. "Your father's here. You're excused."

His father was pacing back and forth inside the front door. He wore his tan work clothes, not the suit he always wore on Monday mornings.

Without so much as a nod of greeting, his father led

140

him down the steps to the station wagon, which was flanked by two cars from the California Highway Patrol. Four policemen sat in one car and three in the other. As he walked past the one police car, Allan saw two shotguns in a rack on the dashboard. Or were they rifles?

Sam, in the back seat, was cringing against the side. In the front seat, beside his father, a highway patrolman lifted his plexiglass visor high up over the swell of his blue helmet.

As they moved out of the parking lot, Allan looked up to see the faces of his classmates pressed against the windows.

His father drove fast but kept a respectable distance between the two police cars, which turned on their sirens the moment they touched the freeway. With a plaintive little groan, Sam slid down further in the seat. Allan forced himself to sit up straighter.

"Your friend, Butright, injured two of my men," his father said. "One pretty badly."

What could those words mean? How could Horace Butright injure two of his dad's workers?

"We'll ask him to come out peacefully," his father said. "Right?"

"Right," the policeman replied.

"We don't want any more men hurt. And we don't want to hurt *him*. When we get there, Allan, you and Sam are going to talk to him. Convince him to come out. You won't go near the house. You'll just talk to him. That clear?"

Allan nodded.

"I said is that clear?"

"Yes," Allan said.

The patrolman removed his helmet. His damp hair lay in flat curls against his forehead. "You think he'll take the bait?"

141

"He better."

"It might be easier . . . and safer in the long run . . . to lob a couple gas shells in there and . . ."

"No," Allan said. "Please don't hurt him. Please. He'll come out."

"I hope he does," the patrolman said. "From what I hear he's no teen-ager. Tear gas isn't recommended for old people."

"I just want to get him out of there," Mr. Collins said, "and turned over to the county. Legally, I'm free to start work on the place today. Right now. The county was supposed to get him out, get him to a rest home. They didn't. Well, I did it myself. I got a rest home all set up. He is now a trespasser on . . ."

"Look, Mr. Collins, I'm not interested in your private legal problems with the old man or the county. That's all your problem. But that man's dangerous. He's assaulted several people, with dangerous weapons. Hurt one seriously. That's what I'm here for."

"I'm covered legally," Mr. Collins said. "By contract I'm free to start work today. I was gonna wait till next week, but I decided to go ahead today. I want him out. That's all."

"Like I said, Mr. Collins . . . well, you think he'll come out peaceful, son?"

Allan managed to murmur yes, he thought so.

Come out peaceful? Where? Come where? Allan refused to move his eyes from the back of the patrolman's head. Sam, he knew, was expecting him to do something, to think of something that could save Horace. Yielding to his unbearable need for an ally, Allan sneaked a glance to his left. Sam, squeezing himself into the bright brown leather, seemed to grow more despairing as Allan watched.

"The county," Mr. Collins said. "The county's responsible for this. Keeping an old coot like that, ninety

142

years old, in a job like that. Someone ought to have to answer for it."

"Well," the patrolman said, "that's the way things are. Never been any reason to change, so why change? The gates open every morning, the garbage gets dumped, the gates close every evening. No reason to change anything."

"I didn't expect this. It's like the war."

The patrolman said well, he didn't expect much trouble. If the boys couldn't convince the old man to give up, to walk out, a few whiffs of tear gas would do the job. "I've seen him," the patrolman added, pushing his hand through the curly brown hair below the lifted helmet. "Couple times I've taken stuff to the dump. Saturday mornings. Hope he doesn't drop dead of a heart attack. Listen, when that marina's finished, I get first crack at the dock sites. I just bought a boat."

"I don't know," Mr. Collins said. "If this is any indication of what's ahead . . . I don't know."

The sign at the edge of the freeway indicated the turnoff for Anders Corners to be one-half mile away.

Allan tried not to listen to the voices in the front seat. The first police car, siren screaming, red light revolving, moved down the ramp marked Anders Corners. Their station wagon followed. The siren behind drew closer. They were speeding along the asphalt road on which, approximately twelve hours before, Horace had been telling them stories about the land . . . the land as it had been half a century ago.

The front car disappeared and then, around the bend, there it was, in the middle of the road, stopped. The driver, a tall, baby-faced policeman, approached the station wagon. The second police car drew alongside.

The patrolman sitting beside Mr. Collins leaned over. "Cut the siren, Paul. We'll ease in from here. Meet you at the gates."

143

Those instructions, relayed to the driver of the second car, stopped both sirens. Then all three cars moved down the road. They passed a yellow bulldozer at the edge of the road, its oil-stained rear settled in the dust, its blade raised and ready. It faced down the road that led to the dump, a tank prepared to lead a charge.

Standing on top of the mud-caked track, a short, fat worker wearing grease-smeared coveralls and a safety helmet was pouring oil from a dented can into the motor. "All ready," he shouted, as they passed him. "Let me know when you need me."

The patrolman sitting beside Mr. Collins waved in reply.

County Dump

Allan's stomach tightened. He tried to swallow, but his throat had turned to sandpaper. He closed his eyes, swearing he'd keep them closed forever, but when the car stopped, he opened them. The charred hulk of a bulldozer, smaller than the one they'd just passed, leaned against the gate. Its blade was raised high, probably to its maximum height, and hanging from its iron lips were shreds of fence and strings of wire. Wisps of smoke streamed out of various cracks and apertures in the charred body. The leather seat where a driver had once sat was almost totally burned away, leaving the iron frame and tufts of some sort of fabric that continued to add its smoke to the general gray pall that hovered over the entire dump.

Four workers suddenly appeared from behind the bulldozer. One of them, whom Allan had seen before, said that everything had been quiet. "The old boy's still in there," he said.

The patrolman nodded in the direction of the house. "Still got his artillery zeroed in on us?"

144

They stood together, the workers and the highway patrolmen, and Allan and Sam and their father, and they all looked across the flat dusty field at the gray shack cowering in the shadow of the redwood tree.

"Damn fool," one of the patrolmen said. "He doesn't have any idea how dangerous that stuff is."

"He knows. Why do you think he's got those rockets pointed right up your ass?"

The workers and the policemen exchanged jokes that described different techniques for bringing the old man to his senses. The policeman who'd ridden in their car and who was obviously in charge reminded everyone that there were kids here and they ought to keep it clean.

The officer asked for a horn, and one of the other policemen supplied it. The officer clicked the switch and raised the horn to his mouth. "Mr. Butright . . . Horace Butright . . . this is Lieutenant O'Neil of the California Highway Patrol. I ask you once again, sir: will you please come out of your house with your arms over your head. We do not want to hurt you, sir. We are here for your benefit."

"You think he'll come out?" Mr. Collins asked.

"Damned if I know." Lieutenant O'Neil shook his head. "But I sure like this whole thing less and less. It has all the earmarks of a messy situation. Ten highway patrolmen against a hundred-year-old man. I can just see the headlines. Win, draw, or lose, the cops lose. We take the usual pasting in the papers."

"Well," Mr. Collins said, "he is occupying private property."

"It wasn't private until last Friday. And no one bothered to tell him."

"But he's injured two of my men. He's burned an expensive piece of equipment. He's disobeying . . ."

Lieutenant O'Neil held up his hand. "I know, Mr.

145

Collins. I know. And I'll enforce the law, believe me. But I don't have to say I like the job. I don't."

The highway patrolmen and the workers, as if by common consent, fell silent.

"Looks like my kid's set of toy Nike missiles," one of the officers said. Lieutenant O'Neil said he wished they were toys but they weren't.

Sam, Allan noticed, was leaning against the station wagon, his hands in his jacket pockets. He was shivering. His face had gone slack, as if the bones inside the flesh had been removed. He looked as though he might be sick. Allan walked over to stand beside him.

Sam's red-rimmed eyes came up, appealing not for comfort but for help . . . for immediate help. Allan looked away.

"Walk toward the house," a worker said. "Write us and let us know." The other workers and the patrolmen laughed.

"Here they are," one of the patrolmen said. "The buzzards."

A green station wagon rolled down the incline and stopped behind the last police car. A large card . . . the word PRESS printed on it . . . was propped upright on the dashboard, against the windshield. Allan saw the letters KRPX-TV on the side of the station wagon. Three men stepped out, one of them carrying a large shoulder camera.

Lieutenant O'Neil greeted them and stopped them with his right hand in the air. "Wouldn't come any closer, fellows. Dangerous territory here. Better get your piss-pots."

One of the men went to the back seat of the station wagon and returned with three yellow helmets, all three labeled, in bright red, KRPX-TV NEWS. Allan recognized the man to whom Lieutenant O'Neil was talking.

146

He was Robert K. Shields, who appeared on KRPX every evening, on the six o'clock news.

"I'd appreciate your help here, Shields," Lieutenant O'Neil said. "This is a delicate situation."

The reporter signaled the cameramen to get some pictures of the charred remains of the bulldozer. He was writing in a notebook while he said, "Mercy Hospital says Jack Donleavy's in serious condition. How'd it happen, Lieutenant?"

"Talk to Mr. Collins here," the Lieutenant said. "He was present at the time. I wasn't. And Mr. Donleavy's one of his employees."

Workers and police crowded close to make sure they were not left out of the picture. Allan's father shook his head. He looked troubled. For a moment it appeared that he might turn away and not answer any questions, but then he said, "Well, it's a simple case of property rights. This land belongs to Redwood County. My company, Collins Construction Company, was awarded the contract to construct a marina here. I brought a few of my men today to start clearing the land. We found this crazy old coot, Butright. He won't leave. He's crazy. He shot about a hundred rockets at us. You can see what he did to one of my bulldozers. It's ruined. Fifty thousand dollars . . . shot. And two of my men were injured, one seriously. The man's insane. He ought to be put away, for his own protection."

"Was there any discussion with Mr. Butright? Did anyone try to advise him about what was happening?"

"That was the county's responsibility. I've got a contract to do a job. I'm not supposed to do their work. And I don't run an old-folks home, damn it. I think he's senile. I think he's dangerous. The county's going to have to lock him up somewhere."

Until then Allan had felt listless, drained of energy,

147

almost defeated. He'd not been angry, he'd had no longing for vengeance. He had been afloat in a pool of dull, overpowering apathy. But now, hearing his father shape the facts so that Horace became the villain and he became the hapless victim, Allan shook tears from his eyes. He would not cry. Not yet, anyway. He stepped aside as the men closed in around his father, jockeying for position in front of the camera.

Allan walked through the smashed, charred gates. He began to trot and then to run. He ran faster than he'd ever run before.

He knew the footsteps behind him were those of workers or of police, but he did not stop. When he reached the house, he turned and saw Sam, gasping, galloping toward him. Unable to stop the momentum of his own body, Sam slammed up against the side of the house. "They're . . . they're . . . coming." He managed to get the words out.

Three policemen, trotting, were twenty or thirty yards away.

The door opened and Horace stumbled out, a box of matches in his hand.

"Stop!" someone shouted through the horn. "Stop! He'll hurt the kids!"

The three policemen stopped. They stood there, on the dusty field, not quite sure what to do with their weapons.

Sam grabbed the matches from Horace's hand. He struck one match and held it near the fuse of the first rocket. "Get back," he said. "Get back. I'll light every one of these if you don't go back."

One of the three policemen took a few steps forward. "Now, look, kid . . ."

Sam moved the flame closer to the fuse.

Allan saw the men at the gate scattering, some of

148

them running down the road, some of them falling to the ground behind the charred bulldozer, some of them crowding into one of the cars, which scurried around in circles in a frenzied search for the asphalt road.

"OK, OK, but you're gonna get yourself . . ."

"Get back."

The three men turned and walked to the fence. Allan touched Horace's arm. "Horace, we told you we'd come back."

Since Allan had last seen Horace, the man seemed to have shrunk inside his own skin. Pale, his jowls sagging, his lips almost lost in a tangled web of wrinkles, he mumbled something Allan could not understand.

Allan clutched at the old man's hands. "Horace, don't be scared. We're gonna help you."

"Allan," Sam shouted. "They're coming."

Two patrolmen with rifles were walking toward the house. A man jumped to the top of the station wagon, and Allan recognized the amplified voice as his father's. "Don't you harm those boys, Butright. You harm them and . . ."

Another man climbed to the top of the car. He grabbed the horn. "Hold it, men. Stop where you are. Mr. Butright, this is Lieutenant O'Neil. You have to understand. Mr. Collins has the authority to tear down this fence. He has a court order, a contract, legal permission to level this dump. There is no more dump, Mr. Butright. Now why don't you just come with us, obey the law, walk toward us with your hands in the air? I'm sure you don't intend to harm those boys."

Horace gazed, sightless, at the source of the voice. His lips were moving, but he made no sound. He swayed and started to fall. Allan caught him in his arms. "Come on, Horace," Allan said. "I'll take you inside. You lie down. You'll feel better if you lie down."

His father's voice drifted across the dump again. "Don't you touch those boys. Don't you take them in that house. Allan . . . Sam . . . be careful . . ."

A muted mouselike squeal came out of Sam's mouth, and he struck a match and set it to two of the fuses. Both rockets blazed across the ground, to the left of the two patrolmen but close enough to frighten one into retreat. His feet tangled with those of the other patrolman and both men fell to the ground.

The rockets struck the fence, sending two geysers of sparks above the gates, or above the opening where the gates had been.

Lieutenant O'Neil ordered the patrolmen to return.

Horace sagged as Allan tried to help him through the doorway. He sat, trembling, on the step. Sam picked his way around him to collect several more rockets from the barrel behind the door. He carried them outside and spread them across the ground, behind those already emplaced. He fixed two in the holes that had contained the rockets just fired. "I'll stand guard," Sam said. "You ought to take Horace inside."

Allan half pushed, half carried Horace into the house. He helped him lie on the cot and then drew the covers up over his chest. Horace grinned a moist toothless grin. "It's Saturday? I slept all week?"

"It's Monday, Horace. Monday morning."

"Monday? I have to . . . I have to open the gates. I'm late." He tried to rise, but he was too weak even to lift his shoulders. He fell back.

"Sam . . ."

That was the voice of Lieutenant O'Neil.

"Is that you, Sam, at those rockets? Listen to me. You don't understand what you're doing. This is very serious. You are assaulting police officers. A serious offense. You almost injured an officer just now. Sam, my

150

advice is to bring Butright out of the house. If you don't, we'll have to come after you. If we come after you, it might not be pleasant. It could be dangerous . . . for Mr. Butright. Do you understand, Sam? Drop those matches now and we won't press charges, but light just one more of those rockets and you'll be committing a felony. Then I'll have to treat you like a criminal. Do you understand? You could go to jail. You don't want to go to jail, Sam. I know you don't. I'll give you three minutes to think about it. If you don't come peacefully in three minutes, we'll have to come after you."

Horace's head came up. "Was that Pa? Tell Pa . . . tell Pa I want to see him." He opened his mouth wide and strained his throat, but instead of a shout the word "Pa" came out as a hoarse whisper.

"Sam!"

Sam came to the door but did not take his eyes from the men at the fence.

"Sam, he's sick. I think he's . . . he's awful sick."

Sam lay his round face on one shoulder so he might have a better view of Horace's face. His lips parted, and the tip of his tongue tapped at the wire braces on his teeth. He started to speak but turned, instead, and ran back to his rockets.

Soft, clucking sounds came from Horace's mouth, and he reached out his right hand to grope for something that seemed to be hovering in the air above the cot. "Hey, Ma's here, too." His arm settled on the cot, and he lifted his body onto one elbow. His eyes seemed to advance and retreat in his head as they gained and lost their power to focus. "Allan." He giggled. "Allan?"

"It's me, Horace,"

"Is it Saturday already?"

"No. It's Monday, Horace."

"Monday? What time?" He fell back again, and the

word *Mama,* as thin and plaintive and lost as the first mewing cry of a newborn kitten, slipped between his chattering teeth.

"They're coming, Allan."

Allan found a heavy jacket on the back of one of the chairs, and he tucked it around Horace's body. Then he went outside, to stand beside Sam. He lifted one of the Roman candles from the supply near the door.

Eight policemen, spread in a long, thin line, their faces covered with gas masks, were advancing across the dump, toward the house.

Sam struck a match and set it to one of the fuses. He stepped down the line, firing one rocket after another. Allan took the matches as the exploding rockets showered the dump with sparks. He lit the fuse of a Roman candle and extended his arm, holding the tube of the candle tightly. A ball of fire shot out of the tube and across the sky, above the advancing patrolmen. He lowered his arm. The next fireball streaked through the air, a foot above the ground, carrying its green flame between two patrolmen, both of whom now raised their weapons. There were two dull thuds. Two puffs of smoke appeared a few yards in front of Allan. The puffs expanded, growing into a cloud that clung to the ground as it rolled and tumbled toward the house.

On the other side of the cloud the workers were trying to move the police cars and the station wagons as two more rockets and two more fireballs smashed into the fence. An explosion rocked the ground, and a mass of flames engulfed one of the cars.

Then the fluffy, stinging smoke poured over Allan. He could no longer see Sam. He could no longer see anything. His eyes seemed to be burning their way out of their sockets. He doubled up, coughing, gasping, wanting to vomit but sure that if he started he'd never stop.

152

He heard Sam calling, he heard Horace coughing. He crawled through the smoke on his hands and knees, finally reaching the cot where Horace, twisting, writhing, was wiping at his eyes and gasping.

"Sam! Help!"

And there was Sam, helping him lift. But they were coughing so hard that they did not have the strength to carry Horace outside. Lying on the floor, his enflamed eyes closed, Allan heard someone shout, "In here . . . here they are . . . quick . . . get them out of here . . . quick . . ."

Allan felt himself lifted, felt himself carried. He was too sick to resist.

When his vomiting stopped and the cool, wet bandages on his eyes were replaced with fresh bandages, he recognized the face of Lieutenant O'Neil. His father, to his left, was talking softly to Sam. "The worst is over, Sam . . . you'll be OK now. . . . Here . . . fresh towels . . ."

"Where's Sam . . . where's Sam?"

"He's here, Allan. He's OK. You'll both be OK."

Allan let himself be helped to a sitting position.

"Allan . . . son, I'm sorry."

His father's eyes were spilling tears.

How often had he been told, by how many friends and relatives, that he had inherited his father's long-lashed, light blue eyes?

The crash of falling timber pulled Sam up from the ground. Allan, knowing what he would be seeing, turned his head to watch the walls of Horace Butright's house collapse. A bulldozer retreated and then charged, crushing its way over what it had already demolished. It charged forward again, striking its blade at the corner of the barn until, with a sigh, as if it had been waiting too long for such relief, the entire structure collapsed upon

153

itself. Still not content, the yellow monster growled back and forth over the mound of lumber until not a single board remained upright.

"Let's go," Lieutenant O'Neil said. He walked toward a police car scarred by the flames.

Horace Butright lay in the back seat of the car, his mouth open, his tongue hanging out, his puffy eyes closed. His head fell back, to accept the oxygen mask one of the patrolmen was setting in place.

Lieutenant O'Neil helped the boys into the station wagon. Their father slid behind the steering wheel. He managed to work the wagon onto the asphalt road, following the second police car. "You feeling better?" he asked. When he did not receive a reply, he adjusted the rear-view mirror so he could see them. He asked again if they were feeling better. Receiving no reply, he turned his attention to the incline that took them onto the freeway.

From the right lane Allan could see the gulls swarming over the garbage. The bulldozer was still ripping away at the remains of Horace Butright's house.

When his father changed lanes, Allan looked back through the rear window. The newsmen from KRPX-TV were standing around the debris.

For a moment . . . for just a moment . . . he could see the top portion of the redwood tree. Then he could see the upper branches . . . then the new green shoots at the tip . . . then nothing.

"I quit," Mr. Collins said. His voice trembled, and he had to make several efforts before he could get all the words out. "I've had it."

Allan lay back, closed his eyes, and returned the wet bandages to his face. He reached down to catch the fat, moist fingers fumbling at his arm, and he brought them, inside his own hand, onto his chest.

154